Praise for Lynn Austin

[An] engrossing family drama against a cloistered, glittering world of Gilded Age wealth. . . . Austin brings a complex tangle of family bonds to life with nuance, delivering an inspiring message.

PUBLISHERS WEEKLY on *All My Secrets*

There's no putting down this nostalgic, appealing read that conveys the feeling of a child's wonder and the building of a caring community.

LIBRARY JOURNAL on *The Wish Book Christmas*

The Wish Book Christmas is a "wise man's" gift to readers as Austin unwraps the true meaning of Christmas. . . . This is a "curl up by a crackling fire with a cup of cocoa" book, a reminder of 1950s America and the reason for the season.

HISTORICAL NOVEL SOCIETY

[A] lovely standalone Christmas tale. . . . This charming book will also be a delight for inspirational readers looking for a feel-good Christmas story.

PUBLISHERS WEEKLY starred review of *The Wish Book Christmas*

Lynn Austin is a master at exploring the depths of human relationships. . . . a beautifully woven page-turner.

SUSAN MEISSNER, bestselling author of *Only the Beautiful* on *If I Were You*

Waiting for Christmas

Also by Lynn Austin

WAITING FOR
CHRISTMAS

LYNN AUSTIN

Tyndale House Publishers
Carol Stream, Illinois

Visit Tyndale online at tyndale.com.

Visit Lynn Austin's website at lynnaustin.org.

Tyndale and Tyndale's quill logo are registered trademarks of Tyndale House Ministries.

Waiting for Christmas

Cover designed by Sarah Susan Richardson

Edited by Kathryn S. Olson

Published in association with the literary agency of Natasha Kern Literary Agency, Inc., P.O. Box 1069, White Salmon, WA 98672.

Scripture quotations on the part-title pages are taken from the Holy Bible, *New International Version,*® *NIV.*® Copyright © 1973, 1978, 1984, 2011 by Biblica, Inc.® Used by permission. All rights reserved worldwide.

All other Scripture quotations are taken from the *Holy Bible*, King James Version.

For information about special discounts for bulk purchases, please contact Tyndale House Publishers at csresponse@tyndale.com, or call 1-855-277-9400.

Library of Congress Cataloging-in-Publication Data

A catalog record for this book is available from the Library of Congress.

ISBN 978-1-4964-7628-9

Printed in China

30	29	28	27	26	25	24
7	6	5	4	3	2	1

For Mom

who always made Christmas special

PART 1

THE CANDLE OF HOPE

The hopes and fears of all the years are met in Thee tonight.

PHILLIPS BROOKS,
"O Little Town of Bethlehem"

Put your hope in God, for I will yet praise him,
my Savior and my God.

PSALM 42:5

CHAPTER 1

NEW YORK CITY

WEDNESDAY, NOVEMBER 27, 1901

Adelaide Forsythe held on to her hat in the wintry wind as she hurried home from the trolley stop. There weren't many things she missed from her former life as a wealthy heiress, but on blustery evenings like this, when the skies were gray and the sun set late in the afternoon, she longed for a carriage and a driver to deliver her to her front door. The meeting she'd braved the cold weather to attend had brought disappointing news. Her efforts to make a difference had made very little difference in the end.

She turned the corner toward home in the growing darkness, plowing through a carpet of rusty leaves. The windows of her modest limestone town house were dark, which meant her husband, Howard, wasn't home yet. She hurried up the brick walkway toward the front door, then halted when something moved in one of the bushes beside the front steps. A shadow shifted, something too large to be a squirrel. She held her breath, listening. Should she run past whatever it was and fumble with the door lock? Or maybe turn back to stand beneath the streetlamp and wait for Howard? He should arrive home shortly.

The bush rustled again. Addy steadied herself, determined to be a brave, modern, twentieth-century woman and not wait for her husband. She heard a muffled sneeze and inched closer, bending to peer beneath the bush.

"Is someone there?"

The huddled shape shifted, and a small face looked up at her. A child! Nestled among the bare branches. A little boy with short, raggedy hair, wind-reddened cheeks, and without a hat on this cold November night. Children lived and slept in the streets in the poorer parts of New York City but not in the quiet Manhattan neighborhood where she and Howard lived.

"I won't hurt you," she said. "You can come out." The boy

eyed her warily from his nest inside the bush. "You look cold. Would you like to come inside and warm up by the fire?" He sniffed and wiped his nose on his sleeve. She thought she saw him nod. "Well, come out, then." After a short pause, the brittle branches swayed and snapped as he crawled out from beneath them. He stood before her, shivering in his threadbare coat, his teeth clacking from the cold. He couldn't have been more than eight or nine years old. "What's your name?"

"J-Jack."

"Let's go inside, Jack. This way." She climbed the steps and unlocked the door, gripping the knob as the wind tried to snatch it from her grasp. The boy followed her as she made her way down the main hall, lighting lamps as she went, then downstairs to the kitchen where a fire smoldered in the cast-iron range. Addy opened one of the round lids and poked the coals to stir them to life, then shoved in several logs from the woodbox. She was proud of herself for remembering to turn the knob on the stovepipe to open the flue. The task of kindling a fire was still new to her. Teams of servants had performed such chores for her until her marriage a month ago.

She turned to the boy, a skinny little child with a dirty face and shabby shoes. His too-short pants revealed bare, bony ankles. He stood with shoulders hunched, hands jammed into his pockets, his cheeks and the tips of his nose and ears red with cold. "So, Jack. Why were you hiding in my bushes? Shouldn't you be home on such a cold night?"

"I don't got a home."

She was about to say that everyone had a home, then remembered where she'd been this morning. Adelaide and her mother had delivered a Christmas donation to the Children's Aid Society's orphanage. She hazarded a guess. "Did you run away from the orphanage, Jack?" He gave a shrug that might have meant anything, but he didn't deny it. "They'll be worried about you. Why did you run away?"

"I wanted to ask the penny lady to help me. I hid in her carriage but she drove away from here before I could talk to her."

The penny lady. "You must mean my mother, Mrs. Stanhope." Mother had continued the tradition that Addy's grandmother, Junietta Stanhope, had begun years ago, giving pennies to the children whenever she visited one of the city's orphanages. But how on earth had the child hidden in the carriage?

The boy sneezed, drawing Addy's attention. After wiping his nose on the shiny spot on his sleeve, he folded his arms across his chest, whether in defiance or to warm himself, she couldn't tell. She glimpsed strength in the set of his jaw and experience beyond his years in his wary blue eyes. Addy knew nothing about children, and wasn't sure what to do with this one. If he'd been motivated enough to run away in freezing weather, it was unlikely that he would want to return to the orphanage, even if she did have a way to take him there.

The kitchen was growing warmer and smelled a bit smoky. She removed her coat and draped it over the back of a chair. "What sort of help do you need?"

He didn't reply. Instead, he pointed behind her and said, "Miss, look!" She turned and saw smoke oozing from between the lids of the stove. Wasn't it supposed to go up the chimney?

"Oh, dear! Do you know anything about stoves, Jack?" He shook his head. The smoke was slowly filling the kitchen. Before she could decide what to do, she heard footsteps upstairs, and a moment later, Howard ducked through the kitchen door, arriving just in time to rescue her like the hero in a fairy tale.

"I thought I heard voices—oh, hey! I think you forgot to open the flue, Addy." He crossed the room and turned the lever on the stovepipe, just as she had done.

"But I did open it. I remembered that I was supposed to, I promise I did."

"I think you may have turned it the wrong way and closed it altogether. But don't worry, everything will be fine in a moment." He opened the kitchen door and used the newspaper that had been tucked beneath his arm to fan the smoke toward it. Addy sank onto a chair, relieved but annoyed with herself. She still had so many things to learn now that she'd willingly given up the life of the idle rich, who had servants to take care of all the mundane household work. Howard made a few more swipes with his newspaper before closing the door again. Thankfully, the smoke was dissipating.

"Who's your little friend?" he asked, studying the boy.

"This is Jack. I found him hiding beneath our bushes."

Howard crouched in front of Jack, smiling his wonderful, warm smile. "Nice to meet you, Jack. I'm Adelaide's husband, Howard Forsythe."

Her husband. They'd been married for all of thirty-four days, and their life together was still wonderfully new. "Before I nearly burned the kitchen down, Jack was explaining that he stowed away in Mother's carriage when we visited the orphanage this morning. He says he needs her help."

"Hmm. It's a little late to bother Mrs. Stanhope tonight. Let's find something to eat, and warm you up a bit, shall we? Then maybe you can tell us more."

Leave it to her brilliant husband to think of something practical, like food. Addy heard him clattering around in the pantry, and he soon produced a plate of cold ham, some pickled beets, a loaf of bread, the butter dish, and a glass of milk for Jack.

"I'm sorry that I didn't have time to fix anything for our dinner," Addy said. "The meeting ran late and I waited forever for a streetcar." Although in truth, any meal Addy prepared wouldn't have amounted to much since she had never cooked a meal in her life.

"It doesn't matter. I had a big lunch with a client." He removed his coat and draped it over a chair, then smoothed his dark hair, disheveled by the wind.

Addy set plates and cutlery on the kitchen table and the three of them sat down to eat. Jack wolfed his food as if he'd been starving. Addy looked up at Howard and made a helpless gesture, asking, *Now what?*

"Do you feel like telling us why you ran away?" Howard asked. Jack eyed him suspiciously as he swallowed a mouthful of bread.

"Promise you won't take me back? Promise you'll help me?"

"I don't want to make any promises I can't keep."

"Well, I won't go back! They're gonna make me get on a train and move far away from here. They think I'm an orphan but I'm not! I'm not!"

"He must mean the orphan trains," Addy said when

Howard gave her a questioning look. "The Aid Society finds families in the Midwest to adopt orphaned children."

"I don't need another family because I already got one!"

Howard rested his hand on Jack's shoulder. "Tell us about your family, son. For starters, can you tell us your last name?"

"It's Thomas. Jack Thomas," the boy said. "There's me, my sister Polly, and our papa. And it's almost Christmas, right?"

Addy glanced at the kitchen calendar. "Yes, in about four weeks."

Jack groaned. "Papa is coming home for Christmas and he won't know where to find us. I gotta find my sister and we gotta get back home before he comes."

"Is your sister in the same orphanage as you?" Addy asked.

"I don't know where she is!" His words came out strangled, as if he was fighting not to cry.

"And your father?" Howard asked.

Jack swallowed. "He works on a ship but he'll be home for Christmas. He promised."

"Tell us about your mother," Howard said gently. Jack lost the battle with his tears and they spilled over, trailing down his dirty face.

"She got sick after Papa left. I tried to take care of her,

but she went to live in heaven." A sob escaped after he spoke the last word.

Addy didn't know what to do. Should she try to hold him, console him? His filthy clothes and runny nose weren't endearing. She wondered about lice. Before she could decide what to do, Howard gently brushed a dried leaf from Jack's hair, then rested his hand on his shoulder again.

"I'm guessing the people from the Children's Aid Society brought you to the orphanage after your mama died?"

"Polly and me tried to hide. They found me but not her."

"How old is Polly?"

"She's three. Almost four. I'm the only person she'll talk to." He swiped his tears again, leaving dirty smears. "Will you help me find her, mister?"

"I'll do my best, but it's too late to start searching tonight. Let's clean up the kitchen and fix you a place to sleep, then we'll see what we can find out in the morning."

Howard washed the dishes and Addy dried them, as they'd been doing since they'd married. "Hopefully, this is the last night you'll have to do kitchen work," Addy told him. "A woman is coming to be interviewed for the position of cook and housekeeper tomorrow. She worked for one of Mother's friends and comes highly recommended."

"Good. I hope she works out, for both our sakes. You shouldn't have to do kitchen work, either, Addy."

Jack helped Howard refill the woodbox and coal scuttle, but when Howard tried to lead him upstairs to sleep in one of the extra bedrooms, he wouldn't budge. "I can sleep down here."

Where he'd be close to a door, Addy guessed, so he could make a quick escape. "There's a little room for the maid, right there," she said, pointing. "But we don't have a maid. Will that do for tonight? It has a small bathroom, too. I'll fetch you an extra blanket." She hurried upstairs to the linen closet and brought one down for him, uneasy with the thought of having a stranger in their home, even if he was a child. She gave Howard the blanket and waited in their parlor while he got Jack settled. The front room was chilly but Addy wisely decided not to try to stoke the fire again. The room's furnishings were a mixture of things Howard had used in his bachelor lodgings and items that Addy's mother had given to them after she'd moved from her seventy-five-room mansion into a smaller one. This town house was small, but it had the modern amenities Addy was accustomed to, such as gas lighting and indoor plumbing. The kitchen was on the lower level, the parlor and dining room on the first floor, and three bedrooms and a bathroom on the second. It was their first home, and Addy loved it.

"Won't the people at the orphanage be worried about him?" she asked when Howard joined her in the parlor. "Should we try to contact them?"

"I don't know of any way to do that, short of going out into the cold ourselves. Tomorrow is soon enough. He's warm and safe, for now." Howard rekindled the fire in the parlor stove as he spoke, then joined her on the settee. Addy hated to bring up financial matters but it had to be done.

"Can we talk about the housekeeper who is coming to be interviewed tomorrow?"

"Of course. What about her?" Addy wasn't sure she had his full attention as he began kissing her neck and a tender place near her ear, sending pleasant chills through her.

"She might be expensive since she worked for one of Mother's wealthy friends, so I've decided that I should pay her wages from my own funds. Once I learn how to cook and keep house, we—"

He stopped kissing her. "Addy, we already decided that we aren't going to spend any more of your inheritance."

"It's *our* inheritance. That money isn't mine anymore. It belongs to both of us."

"Be reasonable, darling. Haven't you and all your friends in the suffrage movement been fighting for financial independence for women? This is the twentieth century and—"

"And I can decide whatever I want. And what I've decided is that my inheritance belongs to both of us."

He took her hands in his and gave them a little shake. "Listen, there's room in our budget for domestic help. I had a woman who cleaned for me and did my washing before we were married. I don't expect you to do that kind of work, Addy. Ever. I'm going to support you. Your inheritance is going to remain tucked away for your future."

Addy decided to drop the matter. She had convinced Howard to use some of her inheritance to purchase this town house, but he remained stubborn about spending any more of it. "Now, speaking of independent women," he said, "how was your suffrage meeting tonight?"

She sighed. "Discouraging. After all our hard work these past few months, it turns out that we didn't help as many candidates get elected as we had hoped to. Only two men who support women's suffrage won seats."

"I'm sorry to hear that. I know how hard you worked and how hopeful you were."

"If women in Colorado and Utah can vote, why can't women in New York?"

"It's very unfair, darling." Howard kissed the backs of her hands, then her wrists. She loved him for his patience with her and for his support for her causes. And for the way he'd

14

sympathized with the raggedy child in their kitchen tonight. "Do you mind that I invited the little orphan boy into our house tonight without asking you? It seemed like the right thing to do."

"Not at all. He would have been frozen by morning." He wrapped his arm around her shoulder and pulled her close to his side.

"What do you make of his story?" she asked.

"I don't know what to think. Hopefully, the orphanage will have more details."

"I wonder if his sister died the same time as his mother."

"Mm. Maybe. It sounds like the father might have abandoned them. If so, someone needs to explain it to Jack in a way he can understand, and help him with his grief. It must be a terrible thing for a child to watch his mother die."

"I can't imagine." Although Addy's father had died very suddenly three years ago, altering her own circumstances. "If his sister is only three, she's more adoptable than an older child."

"I thought the authorities didn't separate siblings."

"They usually don't. But if she and Jack weren't found together, maybe they didn't realize he had a sibling. I want to help him, but where do we begin? This city is so huge it seems like an impossible task to find a lost child and a missing father."

"We'll just do the best we can. After all, we fell in love while searching for your long-lost relative, remember?" She did. And Addy's grandmother had been reunited with her missing son before she'd passed away. Howard began nuzzling her neck again, sending chills of delight all the way to her toes.

"What do you say we head up to bed a little early tonight, Mrs. Forsythe?" he murmured. She smiled up at him.

"I say yes, indeed, Mr. Forsythe."

CHAPTER 2

Adelaide went down to the kitchen the next morning, while Howard was shaving, and peeked into the maid's room. Jack was gone! The bed looked unused, the extra blanket neatly folded. The back door was still bolted from the inside, so he had to be in the house somewhere.

"Jack? Jack, where are you?" She searched the kitchen and the pantry before deciding to fix breakfast, hoping he would appear when he smelled food. She stoked the kitchen stove and added fuel—opening the flue correctly, this time—and was pleased when the embers caught fire. Addy had mastered tea and toast this past month, and by the time the teakettle boiled, she had filled the rack with toasted bread. She poured water and tea leaves into the teapot, turned to set it on the table—and there stood Jack. "Oh! I wondered what happened to you."

"I was hiding."

"Why?" She spread strawberry jam on a piece of toast and handed it to him. He perched on the edge of a chair as if prepared to run as he bit into the bread. "Why were you hiding, Jack?"

"In case they came and tried to take me back there."

"I see. Well, we haven't contacted the orphanage yet, but we'll have to do it later today. Do you like porridge? I can try to make some." Before Jack could reply, Howard strode through the kitchen door, remembering to duck. He had bumped his head on the lintel a few times before learning that the doorframe had been built for maidservants, not men of his height.

"How about some bacon and eggs, instead?" he asked. In a few easy motions he draped his suitcoat over a chair, took down the cast-iron frying pan, layered the bottom of it with bacon from the icebox, and set it on the stove. He'd lived alone before they were married and was much better at domestic life than Adelaide was.

"Won't you be late for work? I can try to finish cooking

if you tell me what to do." The skeptical look he gave her, with one eyebrow raised, made her smile. "Well, I have to learn sooner or later."

"This won't take long." The bacon was already sizzling. Jack watched Howard's movements as the wonderful aroma filled the air. Addy watched him as well, determined to learn from him. Howard cracked two eggs into a bowl and beat them with a fork while the bacon cooked, pausing to sip from the cup of tea Addy had poured for him. "Would you like some eggs too, darling?" he asked.

"No, thank you."

When he finished, he handed the plate to Jack while crunching into an extra piece of bacon. "How old are you, Jack?"

"Eight." His left arm encircled the plate protectively as if expecting someone to snatch it away if he didn't hurry.

"And you said your sister was almost four?"

"She'll only talk to me. Nobody else."

"Why is that?" Jack didn't reply. "Do you know where you lived before you went to the orphanage?"

Jack hesitated as if deciding something, then bent to shovel the rest of his eggs into his mouth before speaking. "In a tall building with lots of steps and lots of people. We had our own rooms there, with a stove and beds and everything."

19

"It sounds like a tenement house," Addy said. One of many hundreds in the city. "Do you remember what street you lived on?" Jack shook his head.

The clock upstairs chimed the hour. Addy pulled Howard's jacket from the back of the chair and held it open for him. "You need to go to work, Mr. Forsythe. I'll figure out what to do about Jack."

He slid his arms into the sleeves and grabbed a piece of toast. "Don't go to the orphanage by yourself, Addy. Try to find someone to go with you."

"I will." He pulled her close for a kiss and she felt embarrassed in front of the boy. She couldn't recall ever seeing her parents kiss, although she knew they loved each other. How different her married life in this simple town house was going to be from her parents' life in a vast mansion. She sat at the table after Howard left, sipping her tea, and watching Jack scoop spoonsful of strawberry jam onto the rest of the toast. She was trying to figure out how the two of them would travel to the orphanage later today when there was a knock on the kitchen door. She opened it to find a tidy, pleasant-looking woman in her fifties smiling up at her. She was dressed in black, from the shawl draped over her iron-gray hair and shoulders, to her long dress, woolen stockings, and sensible work shoes.

"Mrs. Forsythe?" the woman asked.

Addy hesitated, still unused to her new name. "Yes. Yes, I am."

"Good morning. I'm Mrs. Gleason. I'm here about the position of cook and housekeeper."

"Yes, of course. Please, come in." A rush of cold air entered the kitchen with the woman, along with a timid-looking girl in her late teens who slid inside behind her. "Please, have a seat," Addy said, gesturing to the kitchen table. The toast had disappeared, and so had Jack. Mrs. Gleason and the girl remained standing.

"I understand you're looking for someone to cook and clean house for you," she said with a smile.

"Yes, that's right."

"Well, I'll get right to the point. I worked for the Jonathan Hall family for more than thirty years as their head cook. Along with various assistants, I prepared all their daily meals as well as food for dinner parties and balls and other special occasions. You can contact Mrs. Hall or her chief housekeeper for references."

"I've been a guest in the Halls' mansion on several occasions," Addy said, "and I'm sure you're very well qualified. The food was always excellent. But I think I should explain that my husband and I hardly require an experienced chef.

There are only two of us, you see, and we won't be doing any entertaining."

"I know," she said, her smile widening. "That's exactly what I'm looking for. I'm too old and arthritic to stand on my feet all day doing enormous amounts of cooking. I've retired from all that and I live with my widowed sister now, so I'm not seeking a live-in position. I'll only work weekdays, but I'll leave you well supplied with meals for the weekends. Mind you, I'm a cook and nothing more. If you hire me, my great-niece Susannah will do the house-keeping." She gestured to the girl, half-hidden behind her, shivering like a frightened rabbit. She had fair hair and a round, wholesome-looking face that might be pretty if her cheeks weren't so wind-chapped or her hair pulled back so tightly.

"I'm pleased to meet you, Susannah."

"Yes, ma'am." She gave a little curtsy.

"Susannah was raised on a farm upstate and has recently come to live with my sister and me. She's never been in domestic service before, so she doesn't expect a large salary. But she's a hard worker, and I'll teach her everything she needs to know. You'll need to take us together, Mrs. Forsythe, or not at all."

Addy had a lifetime of experience with maids and

domestic servants, and recognized a wonderful opportunity when she saw it. Mrs. Gleason struck her as the type of woman who was sensible and levelheaded, a woman you could turn to in a crisis and trust to be calm and efficient. Her smiles were warm, and judging by her smooth brow, frowning didn't seem to be part of her nature. "The job is yours, Mrs. Gleason. I feel fortunate to have you and Susannah."

"Very well," she said with a brisk nod. "We'll get started right away." She removed her shawl, and pulled a starched white apron from her bag. She prodded Susannah to do the same.

"Oh! I wasn't expecting you to start today."

"Why ever not? We're already here, aren't we? We'll go over some menu plans and I'll purchase groceries later this morning. Susannah, those breakfast dishes aren't going to wash themselves, and—hello! Who is this?"

Jack had reappeared as silently as he had disappeared and stood in the kitchen doorway, appraising the women. "This is Jack. He stowed away in my mother's carriage yesterday when we visited the orphanage where he lives. We're going back there later this morning to sort things out." The boy looked ready to bolt again, but Mrs. Gleason reached out with surprising speed and grasped his collar.

"Very well, Mrs. Forsythe. You may get on about your

day and leave everything to us. Susannah will see that Jack is properly scrubbed and combed and ready to leave when you are."

Addy battled mixed feelings as she made her way upstairs to get dressed. She knew how fortunate she was to have such a capable, experienced servant as Mrs. Gleason. Between her and Susannah, the household's domestic needs would be taken care of without Addy giving them a second thought, just as they had been her entire life. And yet . . . she had recognized the shallow emptiness of that way of life in her parents' vast mansion and had determined to begin again, living a more purposeful life with Howard. He had been raised modestly, a minister's son, with a mother who could run a household, raise children, and still find time for meaningful charity work. Addy longed to be like her, to do everything herself, to make Howard proud. But how would she ever learn to be the wife he needed if servants did all the cooking and cleaning for her? She would have to convince Mrs. Gleason to teach her how to cook and to run the household while she was teaching Susannah.

As for her trip to the orphanage today, it would be difficult and dangerous to travel by streetcar all the way there, so Addy decided that she and Jack would take a trolley to her mother's mansion and ask to borrow her carriage and driver for the trip. At least, that was her plan. When it was time to leave, Jack was nowhere to be found.

"But—he was right here a moment ago," Susannah said. "He just disappeared!" Addy called his name, and she and Susannah searched everywhere for him with no luck.

"He's a slippery little thing, isn't he?" Mrs. Gleason said. "And very good at hiding, I'll give him that."

Adelaide had no choice but to leave without him, determined to accomplish something today. Perhaps the authorities from the orphanage could come back to collect him later. She traveled uptown and found her mother in her mansion's morning room, sipping coffee. Addy sat down to explain everything that had transpired as the maid fetched her a cup. "Jack made it pretty clear that he didn't want to go back to the orphanage," she finished. "He's worried that he'll be selected for one of the orphan trains. I've decided to go to the orphanage without him and try to get this straightened out. May I borrow your carriage and driver for the morning?"

"If you wait for me to get dressed, I'll go with you."

"You don't have to do that."

"I know. But the Stanhope Foundation supports several orphanages in this city, so it concerns me that siblings are being separated or sent away for adoption when they have families."

A short time later, they were on their way. "I'll be glad when Howard and I can afford our own carriage," Addy sighed. "It's another inconvenience that I'm unaccustomed to, but for now, the expense of a horse, carriage, and driver just isn't affordable on Howard's salary."

"I know how much you love Howard," Mother said. "And you're wise not to injure his pride by wanting more than he can afford."

"But why can't a woman contribute more money to the household expenses than her husband does? That's the kind of backward thinking that the suffrage movement is trying so hard to change. At least we've made some progress since the days when a woman wasn't even allowed to own her own property. Before that law was changed, my entire inheritance would have become Howard's when we married. I feel as though that money belongs to both of us, but Howard insists that it's still mine."

"There are many decisions that newlyweds need to work out, dear. You must try to be patient."

Feathery snowflakes were sifting from the sky when Addy and her mother arrived at the Children's Aid Society. The director, Mr. Drayton, seemed surprised to see them again, but quickly made time for them, inviting them into his office. The special treatment wasn't unusual since Mother was chairwoman of the Stanhope Foundation, one of New York's largest charitable organizations, and a supporter of the Children's Aid Society.

"Mrs. Stanhope, Mrs. Forsythe. What brings you back so soon?"

"One of your wards, Jack Thomas, stowed away in my carriage when we were here yesterday. Adelaide found him shivering beneath her bushes last night."

"Well, that's a relief! We were worried when we discovered he was missing. Did you bring him back with you?"

"He's at my town house," Addy said. "He spent the night with us, then hid when I was ready to leave. He told my husband and me quite a story, which we weren't sure was true. I wonder if you could tell us what you know about Jack?"

"I have his file right here. We got it out when he went missing yesterday to see if we could figure out where he might have gone." Mr. Drayton put on a pair of spectacles and opened a folder, taking a moment to look it over. "It seems Jack's mother died of dysentery about a month ago. The building superintendent contacted the police, who contacted us. There were no clues about any other relatives and no sign of his father. The neighbors said they hadn't seen him for several months. We had to assume he'd abandoned the family."

"Jack insists that his father is working on a ship and will be coming home for Christmas. And he claims he has a three-year-old sister named Polly." Mr. Drayton studied the file again.

"There's no record of a sister."

"Might she also have died?"

He shifted a few more papers. "There's nothing about a child's death in the police report. Only the death of the mother, Krystyna Thomas, and her burial in a pauper's grave. It seems young Jack put up a fight when they brought him here. I'm sorry, but there's nothing in the report about a sister."

"Could she have gone to an institution for younger children?" Mother asked.

"It's possible. But it's not uncommon for children who have been through trauma to create imaginary siblings or friends so they don't feel quite as alone. If he had a sister, we would have worked hard to keep them together."

Addy had to admit Polly could be a figment of Jack's imagination. But she wasn't quite ready to give up the search. "Supposing she was found later, where might she have been taken?"

"You might check with the police in that precinct," Mr. Drayton suggested.

"May we have Jack's last known address?" Addy asked.

"Of course. I'll write it down for you. The tenement is not in a very nice part of town. I don't recommend you ladies go there by yourselves." He scribbled the address on a piece of paper.

"When was Jack brought to the orphanage?" Addy asked after he'd handed it to her.

"Let's see . . . on October twenty-sixth of this year." It was the day Addy and Howard had married.

"Will you be bringing Jack back later today?" Mr. Drayton asked.

Addy hesitated. "I'm not sure we'll be very successful with that. He refuses to return, saying he doesn't want to end up on an orphan train."

"Oh, there'll be no more trains until next spring," he said. "But I'm sure you ladies will agree that placing children in homes with families is much more humane than institutionalizing them in orphanages."

"Yes, I do agree," Addy said. She made a quick decision. "Would it be possible for him to stay with my husband and me until we learn more about his father and sister?" She hadn't thought it through ahead of time and hoped she wouldn't regret it later. "It's just that Jack has threatened to run away again if we bring him back here, and I fear he won't survive the freezing temperatures."

Mr. Drayton frowned, removing his spectacles. "You may do so if you wish, but I don't recommend it, Mrs. Forsythe. These children can be very manipulative, playing on your heartstrings to get their own way. And keep in mind he'll be missing school. I'm sure you agree that education is the key to a better future for our orphans."

"I'll make sure he studies every day. Jack seems quite bright." Adelaide could tell by Mr. Drayton's wrinkled brow that he wasn't happy with her decision. Mother asked a few more questions about the orphan trains, the orphanage's policy regarding siblings, and how exactly Jack had been able to slip away from their care. A few minutes later, they said their goodbyes.

"I should have talked it over with Howard before offering to let Jack stay with us," Addy worried on the way home. "I don't know what I was thinking. I don't know anything about caring for a child."

"I don't think Howard will mind, do you? He has a very big heart."

"That's true." Howard was eager to start a family of their own, but the idea terrified Addy. "It's just that Howard and I have so many other things to learn about each other, and I still don't know anything about running a household, and now it seems I've taken on the responsibility for a little boy."

"Don't be too hard on yourself, Addy. Give it time."

"How will we ever find his sister—if she even exists? There must be a dozen orphans' homes in the city."

"I can give you the addresses of the ones our charity supports. If the girl is only three years old, she may not have been able to tell the authorities very much about her family."

"Jack keeps saying that she won't talk to anyone but him—or something like that. Do you really think she might be imaginary?"

Mother laughed. "Wouldn't that be something? I suppose it's possible." They were nearly to Addy's town house when Mother said, "By the way, how was your big suffrage meeting last night?"

"We didn't meet our election goals despite all our hard work. It's so discouraging."

"You're fighting centuries of entrenched beliefs and misconceptions about women's roles and abilities. But think of the progress your grandmother was able to make in her lifetime, founding and running a major charitable foundation. You and I are building on her achievements."

"Are you busy, Mother?" Addy asked when the carriage halted in front of her town house. "Come in and meet our new cook and maidservant. I think they're going to work out very well. And you can meet Jack, if he'll come out of hiding. I would like to hear your opinion of him."

Mother agreed, and Mrs. Gleason, who had already done the shopping, prepared a light lunch for them. Jack had reappeared, and had been bathed and scrubbed clean, something Addy hadn't thought to do last night. He was presented to them with his hair neatly combed and Susannah's firm hand on his shoulder.

"You're the penny lady!" Jack said when he saw Mother.

"Yes, I suppose I am. How do you do, Jack. I understand you've run away from the orphans' home. Is it really so terrible there?"

"They send kids away on a train and nobody ever sees them again."

"But those children will have new homes with good families to take care of them. They'll be much happier in a real home than in the orphanage, don't you think?"

"I already got a family. After I find Polly, we can go home and wait for Papa. He's coming home for Christmas."

"What does Polly look like?" Addy asked, wondering again if she was imaginary. Jack shrugged, then held out his hand, three feet from the floor.

"She's little. With brown hair like mine."

"And you said she'll only talk to you? Why is that?"

Jack shrugged again as if the question was silly. "Because I understand her."

Addy sighed. "We just had a conversation with the director of the orphanage. They've been very worried about you."

"Did you tell them I ain't an orphan?"

"They believe you are. We've agreed to let you stay here with us, for now. But listen, it was naughty of you to run away and cause the people who care about you to worry. If you want our help, you'll need to stop running away and hiding from us. You can't keep disappearing, and it's too cold to be wandering around outside on the streets. Understand?"

"Yes, ma'am." He looked chastened, but only for a moment. "Papa will keep his promise, I know he will." Addy and her mother exchanged looks.

Mrs. Gleason served lunch upstairs in the dining room, and it seemed like a page from Addy's former life as she dined with her mother on the fine, gold-rimmed plates and silver tableware she and Howard had received for wedding presents. Jack, who ate in the kitchen, was intrigued with the hand-cranked dumbwaiter that carried food up to the dining room. Susannah promised to let him crank it once again to return the dishes to the kitchen.

"I don't know where to begin with Jack," Addy whispered

when they'd finished their meal. "I've promised to tutor him, another task I know nothing about."

Mother seemed amused by her worries. "It looks like he could use some new clothes and a decent pair of shoes. Dixon's Department Store would be a good place to start, I should think. I'll send you that list of orphanages when I get home. Let me know how you fare with your search."

Adelaide was waiting in the front hallway when Howard returned home from work that evening. He pulled her into his arms and kissed her before she had time to warn him that their new maid might be nearby. When they pulled apart, he sniffed the air. "Something smells good. Have you been cooking?"

"I hired a cook today, remember? Mrs. Gleason prepared dinner for us tonight."

"Great. I hope it tastes as wonderful as it smells."

"It should. She's a very experienced cook. And her niece, Susannah, is going to do all the cleaning and housekeeping." He looked a bit surprised, so she hurried to finish. "I hope you don't mind that I hired both of them, or that they'll cost a bit more than one servant would have—"

"I trust your judgment, darling. Are they still here? I would like to meet them."

"If you hurry and wash up and change your clothes, they'll serve our dinner right away."

On his way to the stairs, Howard peered into the dining room where Susannah had set the table with a linen cloth, napkins, and their best dinnerware. "My, my! Looks like we're dining in style. Shall I put on my tuxedo?"

She gave him a playful nudge. "Don't be silly. It's just that Mrs. Gleason used to be the head cook in a mansion, and I think she wanted to make a good impression on her first day."

This merging of two lives was proving to be very complicated. Would Howard think she was being pretentious by hiring two servants, trying to live the way she had as a spoiled heiress instead of as his wife? Maybe she should have said no to Mrs. Gleason and hired a single, ordinary housekeeper as she and Howard had agreed in the first place.

Addy was still fretting after she'd introduced the servants to Howard, and the two of them sat down together for dinner. She held her breath as she watched him taste the food and was relieved when he raved about it. "This is better than a fancy restaurant, Addy. You made a great choice."

Addy felt a glow of pride that Howard agreed with her decision. "I'm hoping Mrs. Gleason will give me lessons so I can cook for you myself—"

"You know I don't care about those things. I—" A loud clanking from the dumbwaiter interrupted him. "Are we expecting more food?"

"I don't think so. Jack enjoys tinkering with the crank, and Susannah promised he could help clear the table."

"Wait. Didn't Jack go back to the orphanage today?"

"I couldn't take him back. He hid somewhere when it was time to go and we couldn't find him. Mother went with me, instead. I hope you won't mind, but I told the orphanage that Jack could stay with us until we learn more about his family."

"Of course. Poor little fellow."

"Mother suggested I take him to Dixon's and buy him a warmer coat and new shoes."

"Good. He needs them."

"I am trying to stick to our budget, Howard, and I know that extra expenses like two servants and a new coat and shoes for Jack aren't included in it, but—"

"There's always room in our budget for charity. So, tell me what you learned from Children's Aid." Howard piled more mashed potatoes onto his plate.

She lowered her voice so Jack wouldn't overhear. "They confirmed that Jack's mother died a month ago, but they don't have any record of his father or any other relatives, which is why they brought him to the orphanage. There's no record of a sister, either, so I'm wondering if she might be imaginary. If so, we'll be going on a wild goose chase if we try to find her."

"Sounds like a lot of dead ends."

"But they did give us the address of the tenement where Jack used to live."

"Good. We'll go there on Saturday and talk to some of the neighbors."

"Don't forget, we're invited to my friend Felicity's engagement dinner Saturday night."

"We'll be back in plenty of time to get dressed for dinner."

Addy took a few more bites of food, then stopped. "Oh, no! What will we do with Jack when we go out? Mrs. Gleason and Susannah don't work on weekends."

"I'll think of something."

She had managed to make their simple life more complicated with her impulsiveness. She needed to make it right. "I'm sorry I didn't consult you before making all these decisions today. I know we agreed to do everything together as husband and wife, but . . ."

He laid down his fork and reached for her hand. "I fell in love with you because you're an intelligent, capable woman who doesn't need my permission to follow her heart."

Tears filled Addy's eyes. How had she managed to find such a wonderful man? She squeezed his hand in return. "I love you so much, Howard Forsythe."

CHAPTER 3

Adelaide sat at the kitchen table after Howard left for work, finishing her second cup of tea. Susannah had washed the breakfast dishes and was sweeping the floor while Mrs. Gleason, who had mixed and kneaded a batch of bread dough already, was in the laundry area teaching Jack how to polish shoes.

"Do you know anything about children, Susannah?" Adelaide asked.

"What do you mean, ma'am?"

Addy lowered her voice so Jack wouldn't overhear. "I never had younger siblings, so I'm afraid I know nothing at all about children. I need to take Jack shopping for a new coat and shoes, but I've never taken a child anywhere before."

"I have two younger sisters and three brothers, ma'am. It was my job to take care of them, sometimes."

Addy was relieved. "Good. Then I would like you to come to the department store with Jack and me. You can help me pick out some clothes for him and maybe keep him from dashing away or disappearing."

"What about my work here?"

"It can wait."

The November day was cold as the three of them headed out together for the trip to Dixon's Department Store. Addy was proud of herself for having learned the trolley routes that crisscrossed Manhattan and for tackling them on her own. They stepped off the trolley in the busy shopping district, where pedestrians and businessmen and probably a few pickpockets jammed the sidewalks.

Jack halted as he gazed around at the noise and bustle of finely dressed women and gentlemen as if he'd never seen anything like it before. Perhaps he hadn't. Addy tugged his sleeve to move him toward the main entrance to Dixon's, where Howard had an account. "Stay close to me," she said, "so you won't get lost." Jack nodded, but before they'd walked fifteen feet, Addy lost both him and Susannah when they stopped to stare at Dixon's window displays, decorated for Christmas like a winter fairyland. One window featured a variety of toys, with dolls and tea sets for little girls, and toy locomotives and fire engines for boys.

"Isn't that something, ma'am?" Susannah murmured.

"Have you never been to this department store before?" Addy asked.

"No, ma'am. They don't have stores like this where I come from."

"Where did you shop for clothes?"

Susannah looked at her as if it should be obvious. "From the Sears catalogue. Or else we sewed them ourselves."

Addy had taken so many things for granted. She and Mother shopped in stores in Paris and London, and had their dresses tailor-made by seamstresses. There was so much she still needed to learn about the new life she had chosen. She watched Susannah and Jack trying to take it all in, and decided to let them take their time, moving slowly down the block toward the main entrance so they could admire all the window displays. Once inside the enormous store, Jack halted again. His jaw dropped and he gazed up and around at everything in astonishment. Susannah also seemed unable to move. "Wouldn't it be heaven to work in a place like this?" she murmured.

They were blocking the aisle and receiving annoyed looks from other shoppers, so Adelaide finally took each of them by the hand and tugged them forward. She knew they must look odd—a well-dressed woman dragging a ragamuffin child and a plainly dressed housemaid through the fashionable store, but she feared their shopping trip would take all day if they kept stopping to gawk. They moved past the perfume counter, the fragrances making Addy's nose tingle, then past a display of women's leather gloves. "Where is your children's department?" Addy asked a clerk.

"Second floor, ma'am. The elevators are over there."

Addy prodded Jack and Susannah forward and stopped by the elevator, waiting with the other shoppers for it to arrive. When the heavy door opened, the pair seemed reluctant to step inside. "It's just like the dumbwaiter at home," Addy assured them. "But it's for people. The second floor, please," she told the elevator operator. Jack squeezed her hand as if for reassurance as the door slowly closed behind them. The simple act of innocent trust brought unexpected tears to her eyes. Howard wanted a family. Addy did too, but she'd been raised by nannies and knew nothing about caring for small children. Still, she couldn't deny that something stirred inside when she felt Jack's hand in hers.

They found the children's department, and a saleslady

hurried over, smiling at Addy, who wore an expensive day suit, cashmere overcoat, and stylish hat. "May I help you, ma'am?"

"My little friend could use a warmer coat. And a new set of clothes. And some new shoes."

The clerk's mouth twitched in disapproval as she appraised Jack and Susannah, who looked out of place. The woman's attitude irked Addy, perhaps because it resembled her own, until recently. "Very well, ma'am. Miss Robbins will be happy to help you." She nodded to a nervous-looking junior clerk not much older than Susannah, and the girl hurried over.

"Here's where I'll need your help, Susannah," Addy whispered. She nudged the maid, hoping she would stop gazing around and remember why she'd been asked to come. Together with Miss Robbins, they began choosing clothes from the racks and helping Jack try them on in the fitting room. He seemed overwhelmed as he tried on pants and shirts and new shoes. His old clothing lay like a pile of rags on the floor when they'd finished.

"We'll take two pairs of pants in his size," Addy ordered. "And three shirts."

"He needs socks and undergarments, too," Susannah said. "And a new coat."

"Right." Jack tried on several coats before Addy found one that she thought would be warm enough. "Jack will wear his new clothes and coat home," she told Miss Robbins. "Kindly wrap up the other purchases and drop his old clothes into the trash, if you don't mind."

"Yes, ma'am." The young clerk's head seemed to be spinning. The supervisor, who had watched from a distance, returned to help tally and wrap the purchases. Susannah and Jack gaped in wonder as the sales receipts flew through an overhead network of pneumatic tubes in a metal cylinder. The final bill surprised Addy. It didn't amount to much by her former standards—she had often spent twice that amount on a single pair of shoes and three times as much for a hat. She had never bothered to look at price tags or worry about how much something might cost until her father had died. She had made up her mind to live within Howard's budget when they'd married but had gotten carried away today. She needed to be more careful.

Miss Robbins escorted them to the elevator when they were all done. "Thank you for your help," Addy said as they waited for it. "You did a very good job today."

She blushed. "Thank you, ma'am. I'm sorry if I seemed nervous. This is only my first week here."

"Congratulations. I hope you become head of the department one day."

"Thank you, ma'am."

Addy liked this pleasant young lady. An idea suddenly struck her, and she searched through her bag for a copy of the suffrage newspaper. "Listen, Miss Robbins, I belong to an organization that makes sure working women like you are treated fairly and paid a fair wage. You might be interested in reading some of our materials—"

The girl held up her hand, her eyes wide with fright. "Oh, no thank you, ma'am. We're not allowed to have anything to do with things like that."

"Not allowed? Your employer can't dictate what you may or may not read. You have the freedom to—"

"I don't want to lose my job, ma'am." She glanced over her shoulder at the supervisor. The woman, who had been watching them, hurried over.

"Is there a problem?"

As unfair as it was, Addy needed to drop the matter, for the salesgirl's sake. "There's no problem at all. Miss Robbins has done an excellent job of helping us. She is to be commended." The elevator chimed and the door slid open. Addy left the store seething.

Once again, they took the trolley to within a few blocks of home and walked the rest of the way. Jack skipped ahead in his new coat and shoes. The aroma of fresh bread met Addy when she opened the door. Mrs. Gleason had set a place for Addy upstairs at the dining room table. "Why don't you take a moment to freshen up," she said, "and I'll send up your lunch. Would you prefer tea or coffee, Mrs. Forsythe?"

"Tea, please. Thank you." Addy needed to explain to kind Mrs. Gleason that she wanted to live an ordinary life, and didn't expect special treatment. But now was not the time.

"My, don't you look smart in your new clothes, Jackie-boy?" Addy heard the cook say as Susannah and Jack went downstairs with the packages. Addy took off her coat and hat and went upstairs to change into a simple skirt and shirtwaist. By the time she came down again, a bowl of soup and a plate of delicate luncheon sandwiches were waiting on the table, along with a pot of tea beneath a knitted cozy. The food was delicious, yet Addy felt uneasy as she ate. This wasn't the way she had intended to live with her new husband. She wanted to be a regular wife to Howard, not an indulged heiress. The wonderful Mrs. Gleason was obviously accustomed to serving her wealthy employers, but Addy would have to convince her that she wanted to be tutored, not indulged.

There was a scrape and a squeak as the dumbwaiter door

slid open downstairs. Addy heard Jack's voice echoing up through the shaft. "Can I turn the crank now, Mrs. Gleason? Is it time?"

"Not yet, child. Let's give Mrs. Forsythe a few more minutes to enjoy her lunch, shall we?" Jack must have left the dumbwaiter door open because for the next few minutes, Addy could clearly hear Susannah telling Mrs. Gleason all about Dixon's Department Store, describing marvels and wonders that Addy took for granted.

"Miss Robbins, the clerk who helped us, was just eighteen, like me, and she told me she liked working there, even if her supervisor is a little stern, sometimes. It must be heavenly to work in a grand place like that."

"The only way people like us will ever work at Dixon's is if we're cleaning the floors after the store closes for the night."

Mrs. Gleason's words saddened Adelaide. She felt sorry for young Susannah, growing up on a farm, then moving to the city to clean and scrub, working in someone else's house all day and dreaming of nothing more than becoming a salesclerk. Addy started to take another sip of tea, then stopped. This was America, where people could change their station in life and become anything they wanted to be. Hadn't men like the Vanderbilts and Astors worked their way up from poverty to become millionaires? Her own great-grandfather

Arthur Stanhope had done it, as well. Susannah wasn't reaching for the moon. She merely wanted to work in a beautiful store instead of washing dishes and floors and dirty shirts for the rest of her life. Addy set down her teacup and hurried downstairs to the kitchen.

"How long have you lived in the city, Susannah?"

The girl looked scared, as if she might be in trouble. "Just six months, Mrs. Forsythe."

"And what brought you here from home?" Susannah turned to her aunt, who was also eyeing Adelaide warily.

"There were too many mouths to feed back home, ma'am. Mama said it was high time I got a job and helped out."

"Listen, I saw you admiring the department store today, and I just overheard you telling Mrs. Gleason how much you would like to work there." Susannah's cheeks started turning pink, and Addy quickly pointed to the dumbwaiter. "I'm sorry for eavesdropping, but the sound carried upstairs through the shaft."

"I-I like working here, Mrs. Forsythe! I didn't mean anything—"

"I know you didn't. Listen, I work for an organization that believes women should be allowed to pursue their dreams. Just because you're a maid now, it doesn't mean you can't reach for a higher goal. And I would like to help you do that."

Mrs. Gleason looked concerned. "Please don't give the girl false hope, Mrs. Forsythe."

"I don't believe it is false hope. If she can learn how to clean and keep house, she can learn how to be a salesclerk. I've worked with numerous clerks in my lifetime, and I believe I can teach her how. You went to school, didn't you, Susannah?"

"Yes, ma'am. I finished the eighth grade."

"Good. So, you know how to read and write and do sums. You could earn better pay as a clerk, which means your future will be much better. What do you say?"

Again, Susannah looked to her aunt. "I-I just started working here."

"And you can continue working here and receiving wages while I prepare you for better things." Both women stared at Addy as if she had proposed joining the circus. They needed time. "Why don't you think it over, and we'll talk more about it tomorrow." She was wise enough to leave and return upstairs, but she hoped Susannah would be brave enough to dream.

"Can I turn the crank now, Mrs. Gleason?" Jack asked. "Is it time?"

"Yes, go ahead, Jackie-boy." Addy had worried that he would be in the cook's way, but she seemed very patient with him.

Later that afternoon, Adelaide called Jack upstairs to attempt some schoolwork. She found a storybook that had been Howard's as a child, and she and Jack sat on the settee in the parlor to practice reading. It didn't take Addy long to realize that the book was too advanced for him. She read the story aloud to him instead, pointing to the words as she spoke them so he could follow along. "Now let's practice the alphabet," she said when they reached the end. She gathered paper and pencils and moved to the dining room table where he copied and printed the letters. It was a slow process. Jack was restless and fidgety, sighing and groaning and biting the pencil as if the work was tortuous. It felt tortuous to Addy, as well. They were still at the table, printing the final "Z" when Howard returned home. Jack leaped up and ran to him.

"You're home!"

"I am. Hey, are those new clothes you're wearing?"

"Yep. And I got a new coat, too. Can we go look for Polly now?"

Howard's smile faded. "I'm sorry, Jack, but it's too late in the day. We'll have to wait until I'm free on Saturday."

"But Polly needs me! We gotta find her!"

Addy hurried over to try to soothe him. "You and I are going to check some of the other orphanages in the city, Jack, just as soon as I get a list." She looked up at Howard, who had pulled her close to kiss her cheek. "My mother is sending me a list. Why don't you change your clothes and relax a bit. We can talk more about it over dinner."

"That sounds good." He kissed her again, on the lips this time, and she found herself missing the privacy they'd enjoyed before Jack and the servants had come. She suspected that Howard did, too. She took his coat and hat and hung them on the hall tree, glad that he could come home to a warm meal after a long day, and glad that, for now, she didn't have to worry about preparing it.

Once again, the meal was delicious. The crust on the shepherd's pie was delicate and flaky, the gravy thick and savory, and the meat so tender it seemed to melt in Addy's mouth. Everything about the meal was perfect—and perfectly discouraging. She wanted to be a real wife to Howard, but it would take a lifetime to learn to cook like Mrs. Gleason.

"With food this good, you'll have to take *me* shopping for new clothes," Howard said as he reached for a second helping. "So, tell me about your day. Did you buy Jack's clothes at Dixon's?"

"I did. And a most upsetting incident happened there. I tried to share one of our suffrage newspapers with the young clerk who had waited on us, and she became very frightened and refused to take it. I told her our organization wanted to ensure that young working women were treated fairly, but she said she wasn't allowed to read things like that. Can you imagine?"

"I'm not surprised."

"Why don't people realize that our organization is about so much more than winning the right to vote? Only one of the original resolutions had to do with that. It's about women having the right to a higher education, and to enter a profession, and to be paid fair wages for the work they do."

"You're preaching to the choir, darling. I'm already on your side. Don't let ignorant people upset you."

"I'm sorry. I know I need to let it go and be more patient. It's just that I'm trying so hard to make a difference but I keep hitting brick walls." Addy debated whether to tell Howard about her offer to teach Susannah to be a salesclerk but decided to wait and surprise him. She would have to tell him how much money she'd spent, however. "Howard, I'm sorry to say that I spent a little more money today than I had intended. The truth is, I had no idea how much children's clothes and shoes would cost and I never thought to make note of the prices and add them up until it was too late. It would have been embarrassing to hand back some of the purchases after I saw the bill. I know we discussed our budget, and I know I promised to be careful, but—"

"Addy, darling, stop worrying. It's not as though you went on a spending spree for yourself. Poor Jack needed those clothes."

"But I spent more than we budgeted when I hired the servants, too."

"We'll figure out a way to make it work. From what I've tasted of Mrs. Gleason's cooking, it's certainly worth every penny." He took another bite of shepherd's pie.

"Susannah went with me today to help me shop for Jack. I think I'll take her with me when I search for Polly at the other orphanages."

"That's better than going alone, I suppose. But Susannah seems very young."

"She's eighteen. We managed the trolley routes quite well today, so I think she and I could take public transportation when we search for Jack's sister, too."

Howard stopped eating and looked at her in alarm. "That's not a good idea. Some of those orphans' homes are in unsavory parts of town. I'd prefer it if we went together."

"But it will take too long if we can only search on Saturdays, and poor Jack wants to find his family."

Howard thought for a moment before exhaling. "Then I'll hire a carriage to take you."

"But that's another expense we haven't budgeted for."

"Adelaide, your safety is more important to me than money. Listen, tell me the times and days you plan to go and I'll negotiate a good deal with a carriage driver."

Addy smiled at Howard, knowing she would be wise to concede. "You are good at negotiation, my dear husband."

He smiled in return. "It's what I do best."

Addy wondered what she did best. She had taken Jack into her home, but wasn't very good at tutoring him. She hadn't known how to buy clothes for him without help. And she should have considered the cost and time involved before offering to help him find his family. She still needed to learn how to cook and keep house, and she definitely needed more practice in sticking to a budget. Worst of all, she had hoped to make a difference by supporting women's suffrage but hadn't even been able to convince a young salesclerk that the cause was worthwhile.

Howard reached across the table and took her hand, interrupting her thoughts. "What's wrong, Addy? You're frowning."

She sighed and gave a small smile. "Nothing's wrong. I have everything in the world to be thankful for. And there are so many, many people who don't." Tomorrow was another day. She would do better tomorrow.

CHAPTER 4

Howard tiptoed into the bedroom and gazed down at his beautiful wife, sleeping peacefully. He still found it impossible to believe that Adelaide Stanhope was his wife—his wife! Often, at various times of the day, he would finger his golden wedding band to reassure himself that he wasn't dreaming. He had vowed to take care of her, to love and cherish her, and he longed to wrap her in velvet, and drape her in jewels, and place her on a marble pedestal where no harm could ever come to her. Addy was a marvelous blend of the privileged rich girl she had been raised to be, and the modern, independent woman she was becoming. She was unlike any woman he'd ever met, which is why he loved her so much.

He sat down on the edge of the bed and brushed a lock of hair from her cheek. Addy stirred and opened her eyes, then smiled at him. "You were up very early for a Saturday morning. I missed you."

"I had a few errands to run, so I thought I'd let you sleep another hour or two."

She rose up on her elbows, looking a little panicked as she glanced at the alarm clock on the nightstand. "I didn't realize it was so late! Where's Jack?"

"He was awake when I got up, so I took him with me. I think he's starting to trust me."

"Are we going to visit his former tenement today?"

"We are. I hired a carriage to take us there. It will be arriving in—" he consulted the alarm clock—"about an hour and a half. Shall I fix you some breakfast while you get dressed?"

"I thought we decided that making breakfast was my job."

"We did. But aren't I allowed to treat my beautiful bride occasionally?"

"Well, since you're such an early bird today, I suppose I can make an exception." She smiled, and Howard vowed in his heart to always make her smile.

By the time the carriage arrived, the three of them had eaten breakfast and were bundled up and ready to go. Jack bounced on the seat with excitement as if he longed to trot alongside the horses. When they reached the tenement, he leaped from the carriage before it came to a stop, shouting, "You found it! You found my house!"

"Jack, wait!" Howard tried to grab him, but the boy was too quick. He ran toward the ramshackle building, whooping and laughing as if they'd brought him to a king's palace instead of a dilapidated building, crammed alongside a dozen just like it. The streets resembled a garbage dump with trash blowing across the crumbling road and piled in haphazard heaps. Gray banners of laundry hung from sagging clotheslines, blowing stiffly in the wintry wind. The air reeked of overflowing latrines and decay. Howard winced when Addy pulled out a handkerchief and held it over her nose and mouth. He should have thought this through better. Who knew what they might encounter inside? "Addy, I think you'd better wait out here with the driver. I'll go find Jack."

"Nothing doing. We're in this together." She offered her hand so he could help her down. The raggedy children who had been playing in the street and in the narrow caverns between buildings raced over to their carriage, quickly surrounding it. Addy took Howard's arm as they plowed through the crowd, following Jack into the building.

The stuffy entryway and airless stairwell stank of mildew and filth. The cries of infants leaked from behind closed doors. Jack thundered up the creaking wooden stairs to the second floor, expertly dodging a broken stair tread. "Watch your step," Howard warned Addy as they followed him.

Jack tried to open one of the doors, then pounded on it when he found it locked. An elderly, stoop-backed woman wearing a kerchief and a shapeless black dress finally opened it. Two small children clung to her skirts. "You're in my house!" Jack shouted at her. "You gotta get out! My papa is coming home soon." She waved her fist and shouted back just as loudly in a language that Howard thought might be Russian. He grabbed Jack's arm and gently drew him back.

"You need to calm down, Jack. You won't accomplish anything by shouting. Besides, I don't think she understands English."

"But she's in our house!"

Howard crouched down and held Jack's shoulders. "I'm sorry, son. But after your mother died, and there was no one to pay the rent, they had to lease your apartment to new tenants."

"Well, they gotta give it back when Papa comes home. It's ours!"

How could the boy feel such affection for this place? The darkened room behind the old woman appeared to be a kitchen, bedroom, and living area all in one, crammed with dented pots, sagging beds, and rickety chairs. A string of laundry hung above a pot-bellied stove, and the single, grime-streaked window looked out at the wall of another tenement. Addy had been peering inside as well, but the old woman abruptly slammed the door in their faces. "What now?" Addy asked.

"Let's try to talk to some of Jack's neighbors. I want to ask them to keep an eye out for his father." They knocked on all the other doors on the second floor, asking anyone who answered if they remembered Jack and his family who used to live here.

"Ask if they remember Jack's sister, too," Addy whispered. But the few neighbors who answered their doors seemed frightened and wary of these strangers in fine clothes. Howard couldn't make them understand what he wanted, much less agree to watch for Jack's father. He gave each of them his calling card, just in case, then headed to the basement to talk with the building superintendent. Addy grabbed his hand as they descended the narrow steps, as if expecting rats to scuttle across their path in the gloom. "How can anyone live down here?" she asked.

"It's certainly a different world than we're used to."

The superintendent opened the door a mere crack, eyeing them suspiciously. "What do ya want?" With his unkempt hair and missing teeth, he reminded Howard of a storybook troll.

"My name's Howard Forsythe—and you are?"

"Pawloski. I'm the super."

Howard positioned Jack to stand in front of him. "This is Jack Thomas. He used to live on the second floor with his family. Do you remember him and his family by any chance?"

"Yeah. He's the kid who kicked up an almighty fuss when the authorities came for him. Fought like a wildcat."

Jack's shoulders tensed as if he was preparing for another fight. "That's because I ain't an orphan!"

"What about his sister?" Addy asked. "Do you remember her?"

"Do you see how many kids we got running around here? How do you expect me to keep track of them all?" Pawloski lifted his hands, then let them fall to his sides.

"Any idea about Mr. Thomas, his father? Jack says he found work on a ship and is expected to return later this month."

"Who knows with these people? They come, they go, they speak every language under the sun. They pay their rent; they stay. They get behind; they're gone. That's all I know. The kid's mother died—and she wasn't the only one who died last fall. That means the rent don't get paid, and I gotta call the cops."

"What about the family's belongings? What happened to them?"

Pawloski's face darkened in anger. "Hey, I can't be responsible for things that get left behind. People go through here like vultures. Take whatever they want. What can I do?"

Howard guessed that whatever money Jack's mother had been living on and using to pay the rent had been pocketed, too. He pushed down his own anger and said, "I understand. But what about any personal items, letters, and things that might tell us more about Jack's family, or any relatives he might have?"

"Look, it's been how long? A month? Anything like that's long gone."

Howard knew a dead end when he saw it. He reached into his pocket and gave Mr. Pawloski his card, along with some folded dollar bills. "Please contact me if Mr. Thomas does return for his family. I will make it worth your while."

The man's eyes lit up. "Sure. I'll do that."

"How can you be so calm?" Addy asked as they climbed the steps to the front hall again. "I wanted to punch him."

"You know what they say about catching more flies with honey—Jack, wait! Where are you going?" The boy had raced up the steps ahead of them and flung open the front door.

"I gotta find my sister," he shouted before racing outside.

"Where's he going?" Addy asked.

"Maybe he wants to check their usual hiding places."

"But it's been a month. A three-year-old couldn't have survived all alone for that long."

The look of horror on Addy's face made Howard once again regret bringing her here. Nothing in her sheltered life had prepared her for this. "Let's hope she's imaginary, then." He released her again and steered her through the door.

Outside in the street, the raggedy gang of children had surrounded their carriage, and the driver was patiently letting them pet his horse. When the children saw Addy approaching, they swarmed around her, reaching to stroke her fine cashmere overcoat and gazing up at her as if she was the most beautiful creature in the world. Howard agreed she was.

"Do any of you remember Jack Thomas, the boy who arrived with us?" she asked. Several children responded that they had. "What about his little sister, Polly? Did you see her sometimes?"

"She never played much."

"My ma says she's not right in the head."

"She'll give you the evil eye."

"Naw, she's just feebleminded."

Suddenly, Jack was there, pushing past Howard and barreling into the last boy who had spoken. "You take that back!" The two boys began to brawl.

"Hey! Hey! Stop it! You can't go around punching people, Jack." Howard braved the flailing fists to pull them apart.

"It isn't true! Polly isn't feebleminded!"

"Get in the carriage, son. It's time to go." He pointed Jack toward the carriage, and watched him elbow his way through the crowd, growling and muttering. Howard gave the driver instructions, then helped Addy inside. Jack sat fuming as the carriage lurched and began to move. He appeared to be fighting back tears. At least they knew that Polly wasn't imaginary, but was there any truth behind what the other children said?

They couldn't get Jack to say another word on the way home. He ran downstairs to the kitchen as soon as they arrived. "What should we do?" Addy asked. "It must have been hard for him to see another family living in his home."

"I'll try to talk to him." They followed Jack downstairs, but he wasn't in the kitchen or the little servant's bedroom.

"He's hiding again," Addy said with a groan. "I don't know where he goes, so it's impossible to find him."

"But he can probably hear me. Jack?" Howard called out, "Jack, listen. I know you're hiding because you're afraid that we'll take you back to the orphanage. But I promise you, we won't do that until we've finished searching for Polly and your father." There was no reply. "Please come out, Jack. You can trust us." Silence. Howard turned to Addy, and she looked so sad that he drew her into his arms and held her for a few moments. When they separated again, Jack was standing beside the stove.

"How does he do that?" Addy murmured.

"He should be a magician."

The boy stood stiffly, rocking slightly, jaw clenched, like he was about to explode. "That lady needs to get out of our house! Papa is coming home soon, and he won't know where I am!"

"I made sure the building superintendent knows you're living with us. He'll be watching for your father."

"We gotta find Polly! She wasn't in any of her hiding places."

"Someone must have found her by now and brought her to a different orphanage. We'll look for her, Jack. We won't give up."

"She isn't feebleminded!"

"Why do you suppose that boy said such an unkind thing?" Addy asked.

"I told you. Polly only talks to me. Nobody else."

Howard looked down at this sad, mutinous child and thought he understood what he needed most, right now. He dropped to his knee and pulled him into his arms. Jack clung tightly, wetting Howard's shirt with his tears. His scrawny body shook with sobs. "I don't blame you for crying. It's hard going through so many changes, isn't it, son? But I promise we'll do our best to help you." When Jack's tears were finally spent, Howard rose to his feet. "Come on, let's rummage through the pantry and icebox and see what Mrs. Gleason left us for lunch." The three of them sat at the kitchen table to eat, but unlike Howard, Jack didn't seem to have much of an appetite.

"Don't eat too much, Howard," Addy warned as he piled thick pieces of roasted chicken on Mrs. Gleason's homemade bread to make a sandwich. "Remember, we have an engagement dinner to attend tonight and—" She halted, looking stricken. "Oh, no! We can't leave Jack here all alone!"

"I have it all taken care of, darling. Jack and I went to see my parents this morning. That was one of my errands. They agreed to let him stay with them overnight while we're at the party. We can pick him up tomorrow when we go to church."

She looked relieved. "Thank you for arranging it. I couldn't imagine what we would do."

"No problem. The carriage will be coming back later to take us to the dinner and deliver Jack to the parsonage."

"Two carriage rentals in one day? But the expense—" She stopped as if not wishing to remind him of their budget. "I'm sorry."

"Don't be. You didn't think I would let my beautiful wife take a trolley to the ball tonight, did you? I negotiated a deal with the driver. Negotiations are what I do best, remember? We'll be taken to the ball in style and picked up again at the stroke of midnight. Then, I believe, the coach will turn into a pumpkin."

"A pumpkin?" Jack asked, wide-eyed. "Can I watch?" They laughed at his earnest expression, and Howard tousled his hair. "It was a joke, Jack. Haven't you ever heard the story of Cinderella?" He shook his head. "Well, I'll have to remedy that. Let's see if I can find my old copy of Grimms' fairy tales after lunch and I'll read it to you."

The dream-come-true story seemed as real as Howard's life when he saw his wife dressed in a magnificent gown for the engagement dinner that evening. Howard's story was a male version of Cinderella. How had an ordinary man like him ever managed to win such a stunning, intelligent princess? "You look beautiful, Adelaide."

"Thank you. And look at handsome you in your tuxedo! I'll be the envy of every woman there." Howard doubted that would be true, especially if they knew his yearly income.

The engagement dinner was for Felicity Rhodes, one of Addy's oldest friends, and stepping into the Rhodes's palatial mansion was like stepping into another world, one in which Howard knew he didn't belong any more than little Jack did. He worried that Adelaide missed this luxurious life she had been born into. He could well imagine everyone whispering that Addy had "married down," the daughter of a multimillionaire becoming the wife of a clergyman's son who was trying to make his own way as a lawyer. Still, he vowed to ignore their stares and whispers and be a charming and attentive guest for Addy's sake.

The mansion had been lavishly decorated for Christmas, with ribbons and greenery and ornament-bedecked trees in the foyer, ballroom, and dining room. He and Addy had experienced both extremes today, from ramshackle tenement to rambling mansion, and he marveled that both were in the same city, on the same 23-square-mile island. In between the extremes were his parents' modest home and the simple town house he shared with Addy. The entire main floor of their town house could fit inside this echoing foyer, yet Howard felt blessed.

"What are you smiling at?' Addy whispered as they waited in the receiving line to greet the happy couple.

"I'm thinking that my grandparents were as poor as Jack's family, and yours as wealthy as this family. How blessed we are to have met in the middle." She smiled up at him, and he longed to kiss her, right here, in front of all of high society. "I'm also thinking we need a Christmas tree, although probably not one as tall as that one. I would have to cut a hole in the parlor ceiling to make it fit." He made her laugh, something he hoped to do every day of his life.

Howard greeted Felicity and her fiancé when it was his turn, and thought the prospective groom looked more like a sportsman displaying his trophy than a man in love. There was no hand-holding or tender caresses or dreamy gazes between them. Even after a month of marriage, sparks still seemed to shower between him and Addy like a Roman candle. "I get the sense they aren't madly in love," he whispered to Addy after they'd completed their greetings and moved on.

"Of course not," she said, laughing. "No one in their social circle marries for love. It's all arranged for them. My future would have been the same if I hadn't managed to escape."

"Adelaide!" A voice behind them boomed. "I was hoping I would see you here." Howard turned to see an elegantly dressed gentleman hurrying toward Addy. The man took her gloved hands in his and bent to kiss her cheek. "You look ravishing, my dear!"

"Hello, Alfred. I haven't seen you in ages. And I don't believe you've ever met my husband, Howard Forsythe. Howard, this is Felicity's brother, Alfred Rhodes." Howard's smile wavered. Alfred Rhodes was one of the wealthy suitors who had courted Adelaide. She managed to free her hands and step closer to Howard while they said their how-do-you-dos.

"I heard you had gotten married, Addy, and I must say I was surprised. You promised to wait for me while I was off on my adventures, remember? We'd planned to go to Steeplechase Park on Coney Island, and to the Polo Grounds to see a Giants ball game, remember?"

"I promised no such thing. But how were your travels into the wild? Weren't you hoping to shoot a moose or a buffalo or something?"

"I shot both. And an elk. I would love to tell you all about it, but Mother is signaling to me, so I'd better go see which eligible maiden I'm supposed to be charming tonight. I only wish it was you." He nodded at Howard and sauntered off through the crowd, leaving Howard to wonder if Addy wished the same.

The food was delicious but there was too much of it. By the fifth course, Howard longed to unbutton his waistcoat and loosen his belt. Trained by his mother to clear his plate, he felt obliged not to waste food, but it proved impossible. He did his best to be an interesting dinner companion as he stuffed himself, engaging the people around him in chatter. He was amazed by how much of it was either boisterous bragging or inane foolishness. Addy couldn't possibly miss this excessive nonsense, could she?

As Felicity's longtime friend and bridal attendant, Adelaide was asked to offer one of the many toasts to the happy couple during the meal. "I wish you happiness, always," she said, lifting her glass. "And a long life of meaning and purpose together." Howard smiled to himself. It wasn't a typical toast, but it was typically Adelaide.

They moved into the ballroom after dinner, and Howard led Adelaide onto the dance floor. He would have much preferred to take her into his arms at home, but she was enjoying herself, and therefore he would, too. He kept an eye on the time, knowing the carriage would return for them at midnight. Again, he was reminded of Cinderella.

"Was it terribly boring for you tonight?" Addy asked

when the evening ended and they walked outside to their carriage.

"Not at all. I wish we could attend parties like this more often."

She cocked her head to the side. "You're teasing me."

"No, I'm serious. I could see how much you were enjoying yourself tonight, and making you happy is the most important thing in the world to me. I know you must miss all of this—"

"I don't!"

"Not even a little bit?"

"Listen, for most of the women there, this life of parties and gowns and looking beautiful is all they have. Their lives have very little purpose. But you and I have so much more."

"Well, tonight served as a good reminder to me of how much you've sacrificed in order to marry me, how many changes you've endured. I suppose I worry that in time you'll regret all the losses that a life with me has brought."

She looked up at him, eyes narrowed. "You listen to me, Howard Forsythe. There isn't a single thing in that mansion that I would trade for my life with you." Her face was lovely in the dim light, her breath frozen in the air. Did she have any idea how much he loved her?

"You look cold, beautiful lady. Snuggle a little closer and let me keep you warm."

Howard tried to sneak out of bed the next morning without waking Adelaide. It had been a short night, so he thought he would let her sleep in. But the bed creaked as he rose from it and Addy opened her eyes. "Is it morning already?"

"Yes, but go back to sleep, darling. I'll retrieve Jack from my parents' house and—"

"Not on your life!" She threw the covers aside and scrambled from the bed with surprising speed. "I won't have your mother believing you've married a heathen who skips Sunday church services."

Howard laughed. "As you wish, Mrs. Forsythe."

The December morning was sunny and mild, so they spared the expense of a hired carriage and took a trolley to the parsonage. Jack looked as shiny and well-turned-out as a soldier on dress parade, thanks to Howard's mother. He ran to Howard as soon as he walked through the door and hugged his legs, making him smile.

"Good morning, Jack. Ready to go?" He started to ruffle the boy's hair, but it was as stiff as straw from hair pomade.

"Don't go messing him all up, now," Howard's mother warned.

"Sorry." Howard tried to pat the stiff locks back into place.

"Jack and I have just had a talk about proper behavior in church," Mother said.

"I'm sure you did!" Howard said, laughing. "I think I have that little speech of yours memorized."

"For all the good it did," she replied with a smile.

Jack sat between Howard and Addy in the sanctuary, fidgeting like any eight-year-old would. Today was the first Sunday in Advent, and as a church elder stepped forward to light the first candle in the wreath, Jack started struggling to get past Howard and out of the pew. "Jack, wait! Where are you going?" he whispered as he held him back.

"I need to light one of those candles for Papa and Polly."

"You can't. That's a special candle to mark the weeks until Christmas."

"But Mama used to light a candle whenever we went to church, and we'd say a prayer for Papa to come home, soon. I gotta light a hundred candles for him and Polly!" He seemed frantic.

Howard held him tightly, whispering to try to calm him as people around them began to look their way and frown. "Shh. You can light one and say a prayer after the service, Jack. Can you wait until then?" The boy finally stopped struggling and agreed. But the moment the service ended and the organ postlude began to play, Jack broke free and hurried toward the altar, pushing past everyone.

"Where's he going?" Howard's mother asked as she hurried over.

"He wants to light a candle and say a prayer for his father, as he would do in his own church."

"Then let's help him do it, poor child." She found matches, and Howard boosted Jack up to relight the Advent candle, which had already been extinguished. He thought it was appropriate that this first one was called the candle of hope. Afterwards, Jack knelt in front of the wreath, closed his eyes, and folded his hands to pray. "Jack told me that his mama taught him all about Jesus," Howard's mother whispered as they waited for him. "He said she went to heaven to be with Him. When I tucked him into bed, he asked me to pray that you'll be able to find his father and sister."

"And did you?"

"Of course."

Howard winced. "I'm not sure we should raise Jack's hopes too high. I have no idea if his father is really coming home for Christmas or not. And how will we ever find his sister in such a huge city?"

"I know, son. But this is the season of miracles. Your

father and I will be praying that whatever happens, it will be God's best plan for Jack. We can leave everything in the Lord's hands."

Howard looked at the boy, still kneeling in front of the candle of hope, then he glanced at his wife. Addy was watching him, smiling at him, counting on him to do the impossible and find Jack's family. He shuddered at the thought of disappointing her.

CHAPTER 5

A messenger delivered the list of orphanages from Adelaide's mother just as Howard was leaving for work on Wednesday. "Look at all of these addresses, Howard," she said in dismay. "It's three pages long!"

He took a moment to study the list, which included a brief description of the work each orphanage did. "It does look daunting, darling. I wish I could help."

"It's like searching for a needle in a haystack! Where do I even begin?"

"Start with the ones that are closest to Jack's tenement.

I'll hire a carriage for you, on my way to work. But don't go alone. Try to find someone to go with you."

He kissed her goodbye, and Adelaide went in search of Susannah. "I would like you to come with Jack and me again, later this morning," Addy told the maid.

Susannah, who had been clearing the kitchen table, immediately turned to Mrs. Gleason. "What about my chores? Don't they need to get done?"

"There isn't anything too pressing, is there, Mrs. Gleason?" Addy asked. "Susannah is a hard worker, and the house looks tidy and clean to me. Do you think you can spare her for the morning?"

"Of course, Mrs. Forsythe. It will be good for her to get out and see a bit of the city. Take off your apron, girl, and get ready to go. Jackie-boy is refilling the woodbox for me, but I'll see that he's ready to go when you are."

The December morning was cold and gray, and Adelaide spent most of the drive in the flimsy carriage shivering on the poorly padded seat, trying to stay warm. Susannah rode with her face pressed to the window, gazing like an excited child at the variety of buildings and neighborhoods they passed. Jack seemed unable to sit still, bouncing from one side of the carriage to the other with restless energy and anticipation. There were endless delays as trolleys and wagons tangled with barrows and pushcarts and pedestrians at nearly every intersection. When their carriage halted for a third time in a jumbled snarl of traffic, Adelaide told Jack he could ride up front next to the driver for the rest of the way. She could hear the seat springs creaking as he bounced with excitement.

"This is it, ma'am," the driver announced at last. A small sign in front of the building read *The New York Infant Asylum.*

"According to my mother's information," Addy told Susannah as they climbed from the carriage, "the asylum cares for abandoned foundlings who are often left on their doorstep. They also take infants born to unwed mothers, and babies who are brought in by mothers who are simply too poor to care for them."

"It's so big!" Susannah said. "Who would have ever guessed there'd be so many unwanted babies that they would fill a whole building!"

"It is tragic. And I'm sorry to say this is just the first of a dozen such orphanages in New York."

Jack's exuberance died away as he slowly climbed the steps, eyeing her suspiciously. "You ain't gonna leave me here, are you?"

"No, we came here to look for Polly."

"Is this where they brought her?"

"I don't know, but we'll soon find out."

Jack gripped Susannah's hand as they walked through the main door. The odor of strong cleanser and bleach made Addy's nose prickle. Children's voices and the heartbreaking sound of crying infants tugged at her heart. She used the Stanhope family name and her connection to their charitable foundation to gain an audience with the asylum's head matron. She was a harried-looking woman in a faded skirt, seated in an office that looked as though it had recently been ransacked. She didn't offer them a seat because there weren't any. Addy began the speech she had rehearsed. "We're searching for a missing orphan—"

"Polly and me ain't orphans!" Jack shouted. He dropped Susannah's hand and stood with his arms crossed, glaring up at Addy.

She began again. "This is Jack Thomas, who was taken in by Children's Aid after his mother passed away. But his three-year-old sister, Polly, wasn't brought to the same institution, and she has gone missing. We wondered if you could look through your records and see if, perhaps, she was brought here."

"Of course. What can you tell me about her?"

"Polly would have been brought here on October twenty-sixth of this year, or perhaps a day or two later. She and Jack hid when the authorities came to their tenement, but only he initially was found and brought to Children's Aid."

The director turned to the overflowing shelves behind her and selected a large leather account book with the date 1901 stamped on the cover. She turned to the pages near the end and ran her finger down the listings for October. "It seems we didn't receive any children at all on October twenty-fifth, twenty-sixth, or twenty-seventh. Two children were brought to us the following week, one a little boy, and the other an infant girl of about eighteen months." She turned the page to the listings from November. "During the first week of the month we did receive a three-year-old girl, but she was with her younger brother. That doesn't sound like the child you're searching for. Another three-year-old girl came to us on November tenth, but she was brought in by her very distraught mother, who begged us to care for her."

"So many children," Susannah murmured.

The matron perused the last few pages before looking up at Adelaide. "I'm very sorry, Mrs. Forsythe, but none of our children sounds like the girl you're looking for."

"I understand. Thank you for taking the time to help us." Adelaide turned to Jack, knowing how disappointed he would be, but he was no longer by Susanna's side. He had vanished as if into thin air. "Susannah, where's Jack?"

She looked around in a panic. "I-I don't know."

"Run outside and ask the driver if he's seen him."

"Yes, ma'am." She returned a minute later, breathless and shaking her head. "The driver didn't see Jack come out but he admits he wasn't paying much attention."

"Then Jack still must be inside, somewhere. I'm so sorry," Addy told the matron.

"He couldn't have gone far. I'll show you around and we'll see if he turns up." They began on the main floor, passing through common rooms and a dining room where seven toddlers sat in a row at a wooden table, eating porridge. In another room, three ladies held infants in white gowns and were feeding them from bottles.

"A little boy did come dashing through here a few minutes ago," one of the women said. "He didn't look like one of our children, and he scampered off before we could catch him. He went that way, I think."

The director led them through the building, and it seemed from all the workers they talked to that Jack was going from room to room, floor to floor, searching for his sister. He hadn't called out her name as one might expect, but had dashed into each space, looked closely at every child, searched in every conceivable hiding place in the room, then bolted away again before anyone could catch him. They finally found him in an infant nursery, peering at the sleeping babies in a row of cribs. Susannah expertly blocked his path and grabbed him as if capturing a slippery piglet on the loose. "You're a very naughty boy to run away like that!" she told him.

"Let me go! I gotta find Polly!" He struggled to break free, arms and legs flailing. Addy wouldn't have been strong enough to hold him, but Susannah was.

Addy's frustration and embarrassment made it difficult not to lose her patience as she confronted him. "Jack, your sister isn't here. The matron checked their records. We'll have to try another orphanage." He finally stopped tussling and seemed to calm down. Addy turned to the matron. "I am so sorry for causing such a commotion. We'll be on our way, now. Thank you again for your help."

Susannah dragged Jack by the arm all the way to the carriage. But as she eased her grip to duck inside, Jack broke free again and dashed off. "Jack, stop! Come back! Shall I chase him, ma'am?"

"No, let him go." Adelaide watched him skirt around the asylum's grounds, searching beneath bushes and peering into every crack and hole he saw. Again, she was surprised that he didn't call Polly's name. At last, he slouched back to the carriage looking sad and defeated. She didn't have the heart to scold him, even though it frustrated her that every delay was costing Howard money for the carriage rental. "You can't run off like that, Jack. If you can't mind what I say, I'll have to search for Polly without you."

"But Polly is really good at hiding. I taught her how."

"Well, we'd planned to go to another orphanage this morning. Do you think you can behave this time or should we return home?"

"We gotta go. I gotta find her."

"Then hold Susannah's hand and do *not* let go. If Polly is there, she'll be listed in their record books. She won't be hiding anywhere."

Jack was better behaved as they inquired at St. Christopher's Home on Riverside Drive and 112th Street. According to Mother's notes, the home fostered destitute children from the ages of two to ten, but they found no record of Polly in their registry. The director, a matronly, gray-haired woman, was kind enough to give them a tour of the facility, allowing Jack to take a good look at the children Polly's age. He didn't find her.

"We'll try again another day, Jack. I promise," Addy soothed. "There are more orphanages on the list. We won't give up." The day felt even colder as scattered snowflakes drifted from the gray sky. Jack held back his tears until the carriage began to move, then he broke down and sobbed. Susannah folded him in her arms and held him close. She was crying, too. "Are you all right, Susannah?" Addy asked as she handed her a handkerchief.

She nodded briskly, then seemed to change her mind as she swiped at her reddened eyes. "No. I'm not. Back home on the farm we used to take the baby calves from their mothers to wean them and sell them. Those mother cows would cry and bellow with grief for hours whenever that happened. It would break your heart to hear them. And they're only animals. Today, when I saw all those babies . . . it was like I could hear their mothers crying for their lost children."

Adelaide couldn't reply. She had witnessed an enormous need today and recognized her own helplessness to remedy it. So many children without parents, without love or a home. They had warm beds and three meals a day, but according to the director, there was little hope that even half of them would ever be adopted. Most of them would never have a real home. The fruitless day left her more certain than ever that the suffrage movement could make a difference. By helping women have better lives, they would be helping their children.

Jack burst into tears again when Mrs. Gleason met him at the kitchen door. "Polly wasn't there!" he wailed. "We couldn't find her!"

Mrs. Gleason opened her arms. "Come here, Jackie-boy. You go ahead and cry, honey. You have every right in the world to be sad. Life has been very cruel and unfair to you." Addy watched with tears in her eyes as the cook held him tightly, rocking him. "Do you remember the little baby who was born on Christmas, Jackie?" Mrs. Gleason asked.

"Baby Jesus?" he sniffed.

"Yes. Baby Jesus. He came into the world to show us how very, very much God loves us. We are His children, part of His family. People sometimes leave us or disappoint us, but Jesus never will."

Addy tiptoed from the room, knowing Mrs. Gleason could handle Jack's broken heart much better than she could. She took her time, changing from her traveling suit and freshening up, in order to give them time together. Then she returned to the kitchen to retrieve Jack, remembering her promise to tutor him. She found him sitting at the kitchen table with paper and pencil and an open newspaper. Mrs. Gleason also sat at the table peeling potatoes, skillfully removing the skins in one long, thin strip. Addy stood in the doorway, watching.

"Can you find the price of rice on that page, Jackie-boy? It starts with an *r*."

Jack's tongue stuck out as he leaned close, searching the page. "Here it is! Seven cents for one pound."

"Ah, very good. Can you add rice to our list, then? You should be able to copy the spelling easily enough."

He wrote each letter carefully, saying them out loud as he worked. *"R-I-C-E."*

"That's perfect. You made the letters nice and big so I can read them with my tired, old eyes. Now, what about tea? You know how Mrs. Forsythe likes her cup of tea in the morning. And I'm sure you know what letter *tea* begins with."

"T!" he said happily.

"Ah, what a clever boy you are! And what is the price of tea these days? Can you find it?"

Again, the eager search, tongue sticking out as he concentrated. "I found it! It's fifty cents a pound."

Mrs. Gleason looked up from her potato peels to pat Jack on the head and saw Adelaide. "And speaking of Mrs. Forsythe, here she is! Can I get you a cup of tea or something, dear? Jackie was just helping me write my grocery list."

"No, thank you. Please continue." Addy watched him add *tea* to the list and knew he was learning more down here with the cook than he would upstairs with her. "You're a natural teacher, Mrs. Gleason."

"Well, that's kind of you to say. I would have liked to be a teacher if things had been different." She stared into the distance for a moment as if watching a dream float past, then caught herself. "Would it be all right if Jack went to the grocer's with me? He can help me carry the parcels. And he's very good at figuring out which coins to give the cashier."

Jack looked up at her. "Can I go? Please?"

Addy smiled at the pair of them. "Of course. But I'm sure you never imagined caring for a little boy when you took this job, Mrs. Gleason."

"I don't mind. Jackie's a little lamb." She rose and scraped the peels into the garbage, then stood at the sink, filling a pot with water for the potatoes.

Addy had been standing in the doorway all this time, but she finally stepped into the kitchen and sat down at the table. "I wonder if you would mind teaching me too, Mrs. Gleason?"

"To write a grocery list?" she asked in surprise.

"No, I mean ordinary things. Household things. Like how to cook and keep house."

She stared at Addy in surprise. "You can't be serious. You're a busy young woman with much better things to do than cook and clean. That's why you hired Susannah and me, isn't it?"

"I need to start learning how to do practical things. I want to be a real wife."

Mrs. Gleason shut off the water and studied Addy for a moment as if trying to read her mind. Addy had the uneasy feeling that she could do it. "Is that what Mr. Forsythe wants for you, dear?" she finally asked. "To be cooking and cleaning and doing a servant's job all day?"

Addy looked away. She knew Howard didn't want that at all. But how could she explain how useless she'd felt living the life of a spoiled heiress, and now as an idle wife? "You said I must have better things to do with my time, Mrs. Gleason, but I really don't. I still pay social calls on my friends but I wouldn't even bother doing that except that I'm trying to win them over to the cause of women's suffrage."

"Suffrage? That's all about voting and politics, isn't it?" She carried the pot of potatoes to the stove.

"It's so much more than that. It's about helping women and children. We visited two orphanages today and many of those little ones were there because their mothers couldn't earn enough money to support them. Jobs for women are so limited, and then women are paid less than men are to do the very same work. Women don't have the same opportunities as men to get an education or study for a profession. You just said you would have liked to be a teacher if things had been different—and that's exactly what I mean."

"Put *butter* on the list, Jackie," Mrs. Gleason said when Addy paused. Then she turned to Addy again. "Go on. You were saying?" She truly seemed to be interested.

"I do try to explain some of these issues to my friends when I go calling, but they only want to talk about superficial things. It isn't very polite to dominate the discussion when I'm a guest in someone else's house."

"Why not invite your friends to come here so you can say what you think?"

Addy gave a nervous laugh. "My friends come from very wealthy families. They live in mansions."

"You did too, if I'm not mistaken. This is a very lovely home, Mrs. Forsythe. I could tell on my very first day that it was filled with love. I've worked in mansions like your friends' for years, so I know how cold and empty those places can be. You should be proud of this house and the new life you've chosen. The news is all over the grapevine that you defied convention and turned your back on wealth to marry for love. Some might call you foolish, but most of the servants I know applaud you. That's why I wanted to work here."

Addy was dumbstruck. Was the fact that she'd disdained a loveless, arranged marriage truly a topic of conversation?

And admiration? She had accidentally overheard two women talking about her and Howard in the cloakroom at Felicity's engagement party. One of them had said, "I heard Adelaide Stanhope is living in a cramped town house in a middle-class neighborhood somewhere."

"I heard the same thing," the other one replied. "But I might be tempted to make a few sacrifices to marry a man as handsome as her husband." Addy had hurried away as they'd giggled and gossiped. She'd put it out of her mind until now. But maybe Mrs. Gleason was right. Maybe she needed to show her wealthy society friends what a good life with a good man looked like.

"Does this say *butter*?" Jack interrupted, pointing to the newspaper.

"Exactly so! Good lad. Kindly add it to our list." Mrs. Gleason turned her attention back to Addy. "If nothing else dear, you can give them hope. You're proof that they can marry for love and have a chance at real happiness, which no amount of money can buy. Wouldn't that improve the lives of women, as you're hoping to do?"

Addy laughed. "I would accomplish all that just by inviting them here?"

"There will always be those who'll criticize you and refuse to understand the decisions you've made. Some might be just plain jealous. But one or two of your friends might listen and understand. I should think it would be worth it for the sake of those few."

"You're right. But how—?"

"I'll help you spread a table for tea that's second to none. We'll dazzle your friends with your wonderful new life. And then you can tell them about the important work you're doing to help women. What do you say?"

"You make it seem like anything is possible."

"That's because anything *is* possible." She opened her arms and Adelaide rose without hesitation and went into her embrace. She could see why Jack loved this woman.

"Thank you, Mrs. Gleason," she whispered.

CHAPTER 6

The clock on the nightstand read half past seven. The sun was trying to rise, and Howard and Adelaide were still in bed. Howard loved Saturday mornings when he didn't have to kiss his wife goodbye and hurry off to work. Today, he would join her in the search for Jack's family. Addy had shared her frustrating attempts this past week, visiting five orphanages without luck. Like the hero in one of the adventure stories he'd read as a boy, Howard was determined to race to the rescue.

"I've come up with a plan for today," he told her as they lingered beneath the covers. "I've thought of a way we might be able to learn more about Jack's family."

Addy snuggled closer. "Really? Tell me your plan, Mr. Forsythe."

"Jack told us that he used to go to church to pray with his mother, right? I think we should go back to his old neighborhood and look for places of worship within walking distance of his tenement. Hopefully, Jack will recognize one of the churches and perhaps his priest or pastor can tell us more about the family."

"I think you're brilliant. You know that, don't you?"

"Thanks. But don't heap too many accolades on my head until we see if my plan works."

He hoped that it would. And that it wouldn't take all day. He would hire a carriage to drive them again, and the extra fees were slowly adding up.

They dressed and ate breakfast, and the three of them were ready to put his plan into motion when the carriage arrived. They crossed Manhattan to Jack's old neighborhood and once again, a swarm of children quickly descended on them like flies around a honeypot.

"Stay here in the carriage, Addy," Howard said. "It's too cold for you to be walking around outside. I'll tell the driver to follow Jack and me when we start walking."

"All right. I'll keep my fingers crossed." Howard saw her shiver. The hired carriage wasn't as warm or as weatherproof as the carriages Addy was accustomed to. Her family's coachman had somehow managed to warm up the inside of them before setting out. Addy insisted she didn't mind. But Howard did.

He climbed out, ignoring the urchins who darted around him, and walked with Jack to the front of the tenement. With his hands on Jack's shoulders, Howard turned him around to face the street. "Pretend you and your mother are going to go to church to light a candle and pray for your papa. Do you remember which way you would start walking?"

"Yes," he said without hesitation. "That way."

"Let's go. You lead the way." They started in the direction that Jack had indicated while the horses slowly clopped along behind them. Howard scanned the sky above the tenements for a church steeple but didn't see one beyond the jumble of rickety buildings and endless lines of flapping laundry. Jack halted twice, pausing to look around before walking again. He turned a corner, then spotted a stately brick church up ahead moments before Howard did. He started to run. "Jack! Hold on! Wait up!" Howard couldn't keep up, forced to watch his step in the crumbling, potholed street. By the time he'd reached the church and had helped Addy from the carriage, Jack had tugged open the heavy oak door and disappeared inside. "I see what you mean about Jack running off on you, Addy. He's fast, isn't he? We should sign him up for the footraces."

The sanctuary had the dusty stillness of an attic. If the building had heat, it wasn't working. Howard could see his breath in the incense-scented air. But it was peaceful inside, and the beauty of the winter sun shining through the stained glass windows made him feel as though he had entered a kaleidoscope. It took a moment for his eyes to adjust to the darkness, and when they did, he saw Jack up front by a display of flickering candles. On the other side of the nave, three elderly women in shawls and kerchiefs awaited their turn in the confessional.

"You stay with Jack," Howard whispered to Addy. "I'll wait to talk to the priest." She nodded and made her way down the aisle to where Jack had dropped to his knees, hands folded in prayer. Howard crossed to the booth, wondering what would become of Jack if God didn't answer his seemingly impossible prayers.

When the last woman left the confessional, Howard slipped inside. He could hear the priest's raspy breathing and glimpsed black robes and white hair through the metal grate. "Good morning, Father. My name is Howard Forsythe, and I'm here with one of your young parishioners named Jack Thomas. Would you have a moment to help us?"

"Yes, of course." They both exited the booth and Howard

shook the elderly priest's hand. It felt like ice. "I'm Father Flannigan. How can I help?"

"I'm wondering if you remember that young boy over there. His name is Jack Thomas. He used to come here to pray with his mother and younger sister."

The priest shuffled closer to the display of candles, squinting as he studied Jack. He slowly shook his head. "I'm sorry. So many people come and go, you see."

Howard refused to give up. Maybe he didn't recognize Jack in his new clothes. "Mrs. Thomas was a young mother from a nearby tenement. She had two small children, Jack and his three-year-old sister, Polly. They used to come here to light candles and pray for their father's safe return."

Father Flannigan had been shaking his head, but he suddenly stopped. "Wait! Was the father a sailor who was away at sea?"

"Yes!" Howard shouted with excitement. Addy and Jack both looked up at him. Jack scrambled to his feet and raced over, his shoes slapping on the stone floor and echoing in the sanctuary.

"They used to come quite often," Father Flannigan said, "but I don't think they've been here for a while."

"I'm sorry to say that Mrs. Thomas passed away in October. The authorities took Jack to an orphanage, and he was accidentally separated from his sister. We're trying to find her."

"Ah, yes. I remember now. The girl was an odd little child. Good as gold during Mass. Never talked or said a word. Some kids get restless, you know? They cry and make a fuss. But she was a dreamy little thing, like she was listening to the angels. Very sweet, but something about her was not quite right."

Howard remembered Jack's reaction when the boys from his tenement criticized Polly, and quickly squeezed Jack's shoulder in warning. "What about Mr. Thomas? Do you remember anything that might help us locate him? What type of ship he worked on? A fishing vessel? Cargo ship? A passenger ship, maybe? Or where the ship was headed? Jack says his father is expected home around Christmas, but with his wife gone, and the tenement rented to someone else, the poor man won't know where to find his children."

"I see. I see." The priest stroked his chin as he pondered Howard's questions. "From what I can recall, it was a steamship of some sort. I believe he worked in the boiler room. I got the impression it was a cargo ship, not a passenger liner, but I could be mistaken." He looked down at Jack, resting his hand on the boy's head for a moment.

"I'm very sorry to hear about your mother, son. She was a lovely woman."

Howard thanked Father Flannigan for his help and gave him one of his business cards in case Jack's father inquired at the church. Then they walked outside into the bright winter light. "What now?" Addy asked. She gazed up at Howard, believing in him to do the impossible and find Jack's family. He had won her admiration and respect when his scheme to find her grandmother's lost son had worked. They had found him and reunited the pair. Addy was counting on his cleverness to do it again. He had to think.

"Jack, do you know your father's first name? Do you remember what your mama called him?"

"Sometimes she called him *deer*. It made me laugh because he didn't have antlers."

Howard managed a smile. "Can you remember anything else? Might you be named after him? I assume your full name is John and that Jack is your nickname?"

"What's a nickname?"

"It's a shorter version of a name, or sometimes a description of a person. A person with curly hair might have the nickname, Curly. My full name is Howard, but sometimes my mother calls me Howie."

"My mama called me Jack."

He was getting nowhere. And Addy was shivering. "Do you remember where your father worked before he went away on the ship? In a factory, maybe?"

"I don't know." The boy seemed near tears.

"He's too young, Howard," Addy whispered.

"Tell us anything you do remember about your father. Anything at all."

Jack thought for a moment, biting his lip. "He was very strong. He used to throw me up in the air and catch me again and make me laugh. Sometimes he carried Polly or me on his shoulders. He used to sing songs to us at bedtime." The boy's voice began to tremble. "His beard felt soft when he kissed me."

Howard guessed that this loving father hadn't abandoned his family permanently. "Those are wonderful memories, Jack."

"Mama and Polly and me cried when he had to go away, but he promised he would be home in time for Christmas, and he said he would bring us something special from his travels."

"It sounds like he loves you and your family very much."

Jack's voice grew softer. "We went to see his ship sail away and wave goodbye."

Howard's heart speeded up. "Do you remember when that was? Was it springtime or summer maybe?"

"When it was hot. We walked a long way and Polly got tired."

"Very good, Jack. You've helped a lot. I think I know where to go next." He boosted Jack and Addy into the carriage and asked the driver to take them to the nearest pier or shipyard.

"What do you have in mind?" Addy asked as the carriage lurched forward.

"I'm hoping Jack will recognize something about the place or maybe the brand of shipping line. If so, I can ask if there's a ship due to arrive home around Christmas, and maybe they'll let me see their employment records and we can find out if they have a sailor with the surname Thomas."

"You're brilliant. You know that, don't you?"

Howard winced. "Don't celebrate yet. There are a lot of shipyards in this city. We might be searching for a needle in a haystack."

As luck would have it, Jack did think he recognized the first pier they visited on the East River, about a mile from the tenement. But docks lined the riverbank as far as they could see in both directions, with dozens of ships being loaded and unloaded on the dozens of wharfs. "Let's just walk along here a little way, Jack, and you can tell me if you see a ship that looks familiar. Addy, you should probably wait for us in the carriage. It's damp and cold here by the water."

She shook her head. "I want to go with you." The wind that blew off the river was brisk, nearly snatching their hats from their heads. The area stank of dead fish and rotting garbage. The noise of machinery and squabbling gulls made Howard want to clap his hands over his ears, especially after the silence of the church sanctuary. Addy held tightly to his arm as they made their way north along the river. Jack seemed to have lost much of his enthusiasm and didn't run ahead of them this time.

"Are you looking at the different kinds of ships, Jack? Do you see a paint color or an emblem that reminds you of your father's ship?"

"I think the chimney looked like that one," he said, pointing to a smokestack that was painted black, red, and white. "And I remember that sign because it has a seagull on it." He pointed to the emblem for Patterson & Sons— a white ring with their name surrounding a red circle with a seagull.

"Excellent! Good job, Jack! Let's go talk to them." They found the main office, which was a hive of activity because of a recently arrived ship. They had to wait several minutes before talking to the man in charge, but at least it was warm inside the office. At last, the manager turned his attention to them.

"I'm Jacob Patterson. How can I help you folks?"

Howard breathed a sigh of relief that the owner seemed friendly. He gave Mr. Patterson his business card, and as briefly as possible, explained how the search for Jack's father had led them to this office. Mr. Patterson was in his early forties and kept gazing at Adelaide while Howard spoke, apparently smitten by her beauty and aristocratic bearing. Howard didn't like having men stare at his wife, but if it helped them find Jack's father, so be it.

"I would like to help you folks," Patterson said when Howard finished, "but I should warn you that we aren't the only shipping line that paints our smokestacks those colors. Our emblem is distinctive, though. And we do have several ships that are due to arrive during the month of December. Because of the holidays and all."

Addy must have noticed Mr. Patterson's interest in her because she gave him a dazzling smile and took over the questioning. "That's completely understandable, Mr. Patterson. But I wonder if it might be possible to look at the employee records for those ships and see if there is a sailor on your payroll with the surname of Thomas?"

"Oh, but there would be hundreds of names to search through, ma'am."

"I understand. This looks like a thriving, prosperous business, and I'm sure you are a busy man. My husband and I would be willing to read through the names on our own, if you'll allow it."

Patterson was so charmed by Addy that he not only gave them his record books, but he even offered Addy a chair. Jack stood at the window and watched the activity on the pier while he waited. He seemed tense and alert as if studying the faces of all the laborers to see if one of them might be his father.

Howard found three men with the surname Thomas in the book he read through. Addy found a fourth in hers. The records gave first initials only, and not the sailors' full names, but none of them started with a *J* for John or Jack. It took well over an hour to peruse the names of all the men on all the ships that were due to arrive this month, and in the meantime, Patterson had gone outside. Addy showed him the results when he returned. "May I ask one more favor?" she said, smiling sweetly. "May we leave business cards and a short note for all the sailors named Thomas, so the right one will be able to find his son Jack?"

"Sure. But maybe I should mention that foreign ships

put into port on these docks and anchor alongside our ships. Your missing man could have found work on one of them easier than on mine. Foreign sailors sign up to work in their home countries and sometimes jump ship when they get to America. Happens all the time, and then the captains need to hire new workers."

Howard saw Addy's smile vanish at the hopelessness of it all. They had reached another dead end. He thanked Mr. Patterson and they walked back to the carriage, where the hourly fare had continued to add up. By now, everyone was shivering, including the horses. "That's all for today," Howard said, masking his frustration. "Let's go home and warm up."

PART 2

THE CANDLE OF LOVE

Silent night! Holy night! Son of God,
love's pure light.

JOSEPH MOHR, "Silent Night"

[Love] always protects, always trusts,
always hopes, always perseveres.

1 CORINTHIANS 13:7

CHAPTER 7

Howard gazed into space as he rode the trolley with Addy and Jack to his father's church on Sunday morning. He couldn't stop thinking about yesterday's futile search for Jack's father. The days were flying past, and Christmas would be here soon. Today was the second Sunday in Advent already. This morning they would light the second candle in the wreath, the candle of love. He thought of his love for Addy, and of Jack's love for his family, and would have missed their trolley stop if Addy hadn't nudged him.

"You're in a daze this morning," she said as they walked

the rest of the way to church, accompanied by the familiar peal of steeple bells.

"Sorry. I guess I was woolgathering."

Howard's mind wandered again during his father's sermon as he thought about the events of the past week. The longer it took to find Jack's family, the harder it was for Howard to hang on to hope. The city was so big, Jack's sister so small, and the ocean Jack's father sailed so vast. It might have been easier to explain these facts to Jack, and for the boy to relinquish hope, if his father had been a brute who had terrorized and then abandoned his family. But judging by Jack's memories, his family had been a loving one. And that made everything worse. Love never fails, the Scripture said. So far, Howard's schemes had all failed. He hated to disappoint Jack. Or Addy, who believed in him.

The candles were extinguished at the end of the service. The other parishioners filed from the sanctuary, greeting one another. Addy chatted with Howard's mother, but once again, Jack insisted on going forward and relighting the candle of hope and now the candle of love. Then he wandered over to the creche with wooden figures of the holy family that had been set up near the altar. One of Howard's fondest memories was helping his father and brothers assemble the manger scene each Christmas. Howard still recalled how the carved wooden pieces felt in his hands, how familiar each of the colorful figurines had been to him. The shaggy shepherds and wooly sheep. The elegantly robed kings with their gifts. The angel with feathery wings. The serene Madonna gazing down at the manger. The swaddled baby Jesus asleep on the hay. And with those memories came ones of warm, family Christmases in his home—reading the familiar Christmas story, decorating the tree, exchanging presents—memories that Addy and Jack never had.

"Where's baby Jesus?" Jack asked, interrupting his thoughts. "He isn't in the manger, and I need to ask Him to help me find Polly and Papa."

"Well, since Jesus was born on Christmas Day," Howard explained, "it's a tradition to leave the manger empty until Christmas morning when baby Jesus will arrive."

"That's when Papa is coming, too."

Maybe. Hopefully, Howard wanted to say. "You can still pray, Jack, even if the figure isn't there. Jesus is listening. He always hears our prayers." He wanted to add *but He doesn't always answer them the way we want*, then decided not to. The boy knelt and folded his hands and closed his eyes. Howard offered his own silent pleas for help along with Jack's. He felt the pressure of Addy's and Jack's hopes and expectations like a dull ache in the center of his chest. He would return to work on Monday, and Addy would visit some more orphanages this week, but if she didn't find Polly, Howard would have to come up with another plan of action before next Saturday.

Jack finished his prayer and they walked up the aisle together. Howard's father stood near the door, speaking with the last few people to leave. Howard waited a moment to talk with him alone. "I'm worried, Dad. Jack has been praying so hard to be reunited with his family, but it looks like it might take a miracle for his prayers to be answered. We'll continue searching for his sister, but I think I'm starting to lose hope of finding her."

"And Jack's father?"

"I don't think he abandoned his family. I think it's exactly as Jack says—that he left home to work on a ship and hopes to return by Christmas. But I'm worried that Mr. Thomas won't be able to find his family when he does return. I left word at the tenement and the church and the shipyard—if it's even the right shipyard. But who knows if he'll get my messages?"

"What will happen to Jack if you don't find his sister or his father? Will he go back to the orphanage?"

The ache in Howard's chest moved to his stomach. "I honestly don't know. Addy and I are fond of him, but I can't ask her to take on the responsibility of an eight-year-old boy. She was raised by nannies and nursemaids. Neither one of us is ready to start a family."

"If there's an answer to all of this, God surely knows what it is. Your mother and I will be praying, son."

Adelaide held Howard's arm and Jack took his hand as they walked to the trolley stop. They would ride it back to the town house and eat the meal Mrs. Gleason had left for them. *We must look like a perfect family,* Howard thought as they walked. *Lord, help us.*

MONDAY, DECEMBER 9

The weather was so foul on Monday, the ice and sleet so formidable, that Adelaide surrendered her plans to visit the next orphanage on her list. "We'll go tomorrow, first thing," she promised Jack. "Hopefully, the weather will improve by then." She spent the morning addressing invitations to the tea she and Mrs. Gleason were planning, but each address she penned brought second thoughts. These were addresses of mansions. Part of her felt embarrassed to be hosting her wealthy friends in her humble home. And yet Mrs. Gleason had assured her that she'd sensed warmth and love in this house. Addy hoped her friends would, too. And that they wouldn't pity her. In fact, she felt happier than she'd ever felt in her life.

She finished addressing twelve of them. All twelve of these guests would very likely come, if for no other reason than that they'd be curious about her new life with her new husband. She was about to put the paper and envelopes away when she recalled how young so many of the orphans had been—mere babies! Like Susannah, Addy thought she also could hear their mothers' cries of grief. She uncapped her fountain pen and addressed three more invitations. Her modest parlor and dining room would feel crowded with fifteen women, but Addy decided to think of the spaces as cozy, not cramped. She told Howard about her plans that evening at dinner.

"I hope you don't mind, but I've invited some of my friends and social acquaintances to tea next week. Mrs. Gleason gave me the idea."

He looked at her blankly, as if trying to figure out who Mrs. Gleason was. "Our new cook?" he finally asked in surprise.

"Yes. I was telling her how difficult it is to raise the issue of suffrage when I'm a guest in someone else's house, and she suggested I invite my friends to come here." Howard had speared a forkful of salmon, but his hand halted halfway to his mouth.

"They're coming here?"

"Yes." She tried to read his expression and thought she saw several emotions flicker across his handsome face. Surprise certainly, obvious from his raised eyebrows. A small, brief smile of happiness that she would like to think was because she was working for a cause she believed in. But she saw anxiety as well in his wrinkled brow, and in the fact that his smile wavered. Was he worried about the cost of entertaining such wealthy guests? Or was he embarrassed for her sake by their humble home? He'd said repeatedly when they'd purchased the town house that he wished he could buy her a mansion.

"Mrs. Gleason has promised to dazzle them with a sumptuous tea," Addy said, when Howard didn't reply. "I'll take money from my inheritance to pay the extra costs—"

"You don't need to touch that money. We've discussed this before, Addy." Now his expression showed irritation, which he was battling to contain. He set down his fork and reached for her hand. "That money is to be set aside for your future. It's your security in case anything happens to me. We can afford to host your friends, even if Mrs. Gleason prepares a banquet fit for a king."

"Thank you." She would say no more about it. They ate in silence for a moment before Addy spoke again. "I can't stop thinking about Jack's description of his father as a man who played with his children and sang to them. I've never known a father like that. Mine was a good man, but . . . distant. It makes me wonder which of us, Jack or I, was the rich one and which of us was poor?" Howard rose from his seat and went to her, bending to silently embrace her.

The weather cleared by Wednesday, so Addy set out in the hired carriage with Susannah and Jack to visit two more orphanages. The first was the New York Foundling Hospital on East Sixty-eighth Street. According to Mother's description, two nuns founded it after the Civil War as a place where desperate mothers could leave their babies.

"You must promise not to let go of Susannah's hand this time," Addy told Jack before they went inside.

"I promise." He squeezed out the words grudgingly.

Addy explained to the nun in charge why they had come, and she was eager to help. She asked her assistant to pore over the records while she escorted the three of them on a tour.

"Sister Irene founded our institution in a modest home in the Greenwich Village neighborhood," she explained. "She placed a wicker cradle on her doorstep, and that very first night, a newborn baby was placed inside it. The need has only multiplied in the years since. It would break your heart to read the notes mothers sometimes leave with their babies."

"Do you think I might have a copy of one of them?" Addy asked. "The suffrage group I work with is trying to raise awareness of the need to help desperate women like these mothers. I think it would open many eyes if I shared one mother's own words."

"That would be wonderful, Mrs. Forsythe. I thank you for anything you can do to help."

The nun led them to a large room with a row of cots and cribs lining one wall. More than a dozen toddlers had been playing on the wooden floor, but they grew quiet when they saw the strangers. The hopeful, expectant looks on their faces touched Addy's heart. She saw Susannah searching her pockets for a handkerchief. She had let go of Jack's hand for a moment, and he moved into the room, laying his hand on each child's head as if in silent comfort.

They didn't find Polly. The record books showed no little girls matching her description. "I'm so sorry we couldn't help," the sister said. "But maybe this letter will." She gave Addy a copy of a note from an abandoned child's mother.

The disappointment and overwhelming need she'd witnessed sapped Addy's strength. Seeing Jack's forlorn face made her glad they were going to try one more orphans' home before returning to the town house. This home was affiliated with The Five Points Mission. Addy had been avoiding the Five Points neighborhood because of its violent reputation, but their driver had promised Howard that he would watch over them. Mother's description of the mission noted the fine work it had accomplished in an area known for its utter destitution and hopelessness. But after a search of their records, Addy was disappointed to learn that Polly hadn't been brought there, either.

They had visited all the orphanages nearest to Jack's tenement, the easiest and most convenient places to have taken Polly—without luck. Now they would have to expand the radius of their search and visit some of the smaller, lesser-known institutions. But not today. Addy could see the toll it was taking on Jack and Susannah, indeed, on herself. She would talk with Howard tonight and figure out another way to continue their search.

Jack retreated to the kitchen and Mrs. Gleason's waiting arms when they arrived home. Adelaide sadly crossed off two more orphanages from her list and changed out of her traveling clothes. Afterward, she joined the others in the kitchen for lunch. "If you don't mind, Mrs. Gleason, I would rather eat my noon meal down here with you every day instead of all by myself in the lonely dining room."

"We would love it if you ate with us, dear," Mrs. Gleason said. "Although Jack will be disappointed that he can't crank the dumbwaiter up and down every day." She winked.

When Susannah joined them, dressed in her apron and cap, she seemed very reluctant to sit down and eat at the same table as Addy, as if Addy were royalty and Susannah a mere servant. The maid nervously twisted her hands and kept looking to Mrs. Gleason for reassurance before finally taking a seat. Did she fear her manners weren't good enough? The distinction between servant and employer had been very sharp in Addy's household when she was growing up, and even now, Mother wouldn't dream of sitting down at the table with her maids. But Addy's life was going in a new, more modern direction, and if she wanted to help women from all classes and situations, she needed to befriend them, listen to them. She remembered Susannah's wish to be a salesclerk in a fabulous store like Dixon's and decided to do something about it.

"We won't be visiting any orphans' homes tomorrow, Susannah, but I need to do a little Christmas shopping, and I would like you to come with me." Once again, the girl looked to her great-aunt, her blue eyes wide with alarm.

"If that's what Mrs. Forsythe wants, of course you should go with her, dear," Mrs. Gleason said.

"You're a very hard worker, Susannah, and you're doing a fine job. You keep our town house sparkling clean. It won't hurt if we spend an hour or two shopping tomorrow."

They left Jack at home with Mrs. Gleason the next day, and took the trolley to the shopping district. Addy hadn't anticipated how busy it would be, the stores crowded with holiday shoppers. It had never been a tradition in Addy's family to exchange Christmas presents. What do you buy someone who has everything? She remembered the holidays as a season of fancy balls and parties with her parents and sisters, dressed in their finest clothes and jewels. Her grandmother had rarely attended any of these events. Instead, Addy remembered Mimi Junie collecting clothing and toys and extra treats like oranges to deliver to the orphanages that her charity supported. She had often asked Addy and her sisters to join her, and Addy now regretted that she hadn't done so, too enamored with her gilded life to go. But her life was different, now. She would give her time to helping others, starting with helping Susannah dream of a better future.

Once again, the young maid seemed dazzled by everything she saw, her steps slowing as she gazed at the beautiful window displays. Addy didn't hurry her along, allowing her to set the pace until they finally reached Dixon's Department store.

"There are so many beautiful things here," she murmured as she gazed all around the huge store. "We used to order everything from the Sears, Roebuck catalogue."

Addy knew the catalogue existed but had never seen one. "Well, we're here to shop for new leather gloves for my husband. But I want you to watch the salesclerk, Susannah, and listen carefully to everything she says. You'll see that it isn't a difficult job. You could easily do it."

"Me?" Her voice came out in a squeak. "I could never work in a place like this!"

"Of course, you could. And I'm going to teach you how. Come, follow me." She strode to the display case with Susannah trailing behind. Addy was wearing her fine cashmere coat and a fashionable hat. The clerk behind the glass counter hurried to greet her.

"Good morning, ma'am. How may I help you today?"

Addy took her time, asking to see several different styles and sizes of leather gloves, putting the clerk through her paces as she waited on her. The well-trained clerk was helpful, cheerful, and efficient, setting a good example for Susannah, who seemed to be paying close attention. Eventually, Addy chose a pair of black leather gloves in Howard's size and paid for them with her own spending money. The clerk boxed and gift wrapped them while a metal cylinder, with the money inside, traveled through the pneumatic tubes and returned with the receipt. Addy couldn't have asked for a more perfect transaction for Susannah's first lesson.

The maid was quiet on the way home. Addy hoped she was remembering what she'd just seen and was imagining herself in that role. "Come upstairs to my bedroom with me," she told Susannah when they returned to the town house.

"What about my work? Don't I have floors to scrub?"

"They can wait for another day. This is more important." Once upstairs, Addy laid out several pairs of her own gloves on the bed. "Now, we're going to pretend that you're the salesclerk and I've come to shop. Can you remember what she said and did? Start by greeting me: 'Good morning. May I help you ma'am?'"

"G-good morning. May I help you m-ma'am?" Susannah was nervous, at first, but Addy tried to keep this first lesson light-hearted as they acted out the scene, going through the transaction until they made the final sale.

"That wasn't hard, was it?"

Susannah gave a wavering smile. "No, ma'am. But in a real store . . ."

Addy realized that it would be one thing to teach Susannah to do all the things a salesclerk did, but another thing entirely to teach her poise and self-confidence. She thought for a moment before forming a plan. "We'll keep practicing and visiting real stores until you're ready, but in the meantime, I want you to learn good posture and how to walk gracefully. I'll show you what they taught us to do at the female academy I attended." Addy picked up a book from Howard's side of the bed and balanced it on her head. "In order to keep it from falling off, you must keep your shoulders and spine straight and your chin level. See?" She crossed the room while balancing the book on her head, then returned to Susannah's side. "Now you try it."

Susannah giggled and her cheeks turned pink when her first few attempts made the book slide off her head. Addy laughed with her, coaxing her to try again until Susannah finally was able to walk the length of the room with the book in place. "Perfect, Susannah! Now, I want you to practice every day until it comes naturally. You can show me the results in a few days."

"Yes, ma'am. Thank you, ma'am. Should I go help Mrs. Gleason now?"

"No, wait. One more thing. Did you notice how the salesclerk always wore a pleasant expression on her face? Come here for a minute and look in the mirror with me. See how worried you look, Susannah? Show me your nicest smile. That's better. You look so pretty when you smile. Now when you're at home, after you've practiced walking with the book on your head, I want you to stand in front of a mirror and practice what it feels like to wear a pleasant expression. Practice until you can do it without looking—and without blushing so much. Do you think you can try that?"

Susannah's cheeks turned an even brighter shade of pink, but she nodded and said, "Yes, ma'am. I'll practice, ma'am."

"Good."

The following day, the weather again proved dismal, forcing Addy to remain at home with nothing to do. It occurred to her that she had promised the orphanage director that she would help Jack with his schoolwork, and hadn't done it. She went downstairs to the kitchen to find him. He and Mrs. Gleason were in the middle of baking something, and Jack seemed focused on the array of measuring cups and spoons that Mrs. Gleason had laid out. Cannisters of flour and sugar littered the table, along with jars of spices and other mysterious ingredients. The fire in the range made the kitchen cozy and warm, and the room smelled wonderfully of cinnamon and cloves. "May I watch you?" Addy asked.

"Your company is always welcome, Mrs. Forsythe." She smiled and gestured to a chair with her flour-covered hand. "Did you find the cup with a one and a four on it, Jackie?

Right, then. That's one-fourth of a cup. It takes four of those to make one full cup."

"Four of them?" He looked skeptical.

"See for yourself. Fill it with flour four times and dump it into the bigger cup." Jack's tongue stuck out with concentration, as seemed to be his habit. Flour coated his fingers and dusted the table.

"It works!" he said.

"Now find the cup with a one and a three. How many of those do you think it will take to fill the big cup?"

"Three?"

"Give it a try."

Jack measured and filled the cups, spilling more flour. "Look! It works."

"Right you are. That cup measures one-third. And the last cup is one-half. You'll fill it twice. It works the same way with the measuring spoons." Addy realized that while Mrs. Gleason could probably bake anything she wanted without bothering to measure, she was teaching Jack about fractions, and doing a much better job of it than she could have.

"You're a wonder, Mrs. Gleason. I can't thank you enough for helping me teach him."

"He's a lamb. We like to learn about a lot of different things, don't we, Jackie-boy?"

"Uh-huh." He didn't look up from his experimentation.

Mrs. Gleason cracked four eggs into a bowl. "Jackie has been telling me about the candles he lights in church. We don't have anything like that in my church. He says the first candle stands for hope—and I know how very much he is hoping to find his sister."

Addy didn't want to say that her own hope of finding his family was beginning to wane. She watched Mrs. Gleason beat the eggs into a froth with a whisk, her hand whirling like a machine.

"He tells me that last Sunday's candle stood for love. And love is all over the Bible, isn't it, Mrs. Forsythe? We're told to love God and to love our neighbor. Yet I can't help thinking of all those little babies Susannah told me about, with no one to love them."

"It's heartbreaking. That's what I want to talk to my friends about at my tea next week. Hopefully, they'll help me try to do something about it."

Mrs. Gleason stopped whisking and looked up at Addy. "Love is a funny thing, isn't it? It seems clear what loving our neighbor should look like, even though we neglect doing it. But when it comes to love between a man and a woman, well, we don't always know what's real and what isn't, do we?"

"Have you ever been in love, Mrs. Gleason? I assume there was a Mr. Gleason."

"Oh, yes," she said, chuckling. "Wayne Gleason. I fell in love with handsome, charming Wayne Gleason when I was all of sixteen years old. My parents tried to warn me about him, but would I listen?" She smiled, shaking her head. "We want what we want when we think we're in love instead of what's best for us."

She beat the eggs for another moment, then said, "Find the one-half cup, Jackie-boy, and measure some sugar for me. That's it. Good job. Pour it in here with the eggs." She gave the mixture a few more vigorous stirs, then leaned close to Addy, lowering her voice. "That's one of the reasons why Susannah was sent here to live with my sister and me. The wrong sort of fellow was giving her the wrong sort of attention."

"I see." The news made Addy more determined than ever to help Susannah, who was upstairs dusting the parlor, to dream of better things.

"Now the flour. Two cups of it, Jack, if you please." She continued talking while she worked. "I didn't listen to my parents, of course. I married Wayne Gleason and quickly learned that he spent a lot of his wages on drink instead of on coal to heat our apartment. When our little daughter,

Flossie, died of pneumonia, Wayne blamed himself and couldn't face me. And so, he left."

She got out a baking pan and a brick of lard. "Grease up this pan for me, Jack. You know how to do it. Are your hands clean?"

He quickly swiped them on a towel, then dug his fingers into the lard, smearing it on the pan as if he enjoyed the greasy mess.

"What did you do then, Mrs. Gleason?" Addy asked, intrigued by her sad story.

"I went to work in the Halls' mansion as a cook's assistant. As the years passed and I learned more and more, I became their head cook. The other servants became my family, and when the Halls had children, I loved them as if they were my own. But time changes everything, doesn't it? The children grew up, the other servants moved on or retired, and my family broke apart once again."

"Is this good enough, Mrs. Gleason?" Jack asked.

"It's perfect. Let's pour the batter in it, shall we? And get it into the oven. Then you can lick the bowl."

Addy saw the love shining from Mrs. Gleason's eyes as she gazed at Jack. She remembered her grandmother looking at her the same way, as if she were the most important person in the world. Mimi Junie was gone now, but Addy was grateful for the love they had shared.

"In case you can't tell, Mrs. Forsythe, I love to cook. I feel like it's what God meant for me to do. When I heard about this position, I thought I heard Him whisper that He wanted me to serve Him here, for some reason. Maybe it's for little Jackie-boy's sake."

Addy nodded and swallowed a knot of emotion, knowing Mrs. Gleason had been sent here for her sake, as well.

The cook slid the pan into the oven and wiped her hands on her apron. "Now, we'd better get this mess cleaned up. Mr. Forsythe will be coming home soon, and I'm guessing he'll be hungry."

"He usually is," Addy said, smiling. "You're spoiling him. He never came home to a nice, warm dinner before you started working here."

Mrs. Gleason went to the kitchen stairs and called up to Susannah. "It's time to set the table for dinner, dear."

"Right away, Auntie."

With nothing else to do, Addy went upstairs to wait for Howard.

CHAPTER 8

The bedroom was still dark on Saturday morning when Howard awoke. It was too early to get up, yet worry prevented him from falling back to sleep. He was afraid he'd disturb Addy if he climbed out of bed, so he remained there, his mind a tangled snarl of anxiety. Eleven days until Christmas. He needed a plan for today's search for Jack's sister, but he didn't have one.

They could visit a few more orphanages like Addy had been doing, but that process had already taken too much time and money with no results to show for it.

That was Howard's other worry—money. With the extra

carriage fares, new shoes and clothing for Jack, and the added costs of two new servants, finances had become very strained. Christmas was coming, which meant even more expenses. Addy had shared her excitement about hosting a tea in their home, and although Howard was in favor of it, he worried about how much it would cost. He couldn't tell Addy to economize. He wanted her to have more of everything in life, not less. Nor did he want her to dip into her inheritance. Those funds would be her security if, God forbid, anything happened to him.

He needed to pray, not worry. And he tried to pray, really he did. But Howard's mind was too disordered to think clearly, and all that came out was, "Lord, help. Please, help." He repeated that prayer until some of the pressure in his chest began to ease, and the tangled strings of his thoughts began to loosen. He grabbed onto one of those thoughts and followed where it led, mulling over what he'd been told: After Jack's mother died, and there had been no one to care for the children, the authorities had arrived to collect them.

The authorities.

Which authorities?

The police? Someone—who was it—had mentioned checking the local police precinct in Jack's neighborhood. Was it the building superintendent, Pawloski? He'd said that

Jack had fought like a wildcat. If it was the police who had taken him, and if they had records of relocating Jack, maybe they also had records of finding his sister. Surely someone would have noticed a three-year-old girl wandering around the neighborhood all alone. She couldn't have remained hidden indefinitely.

But what if she had died?

Perhaps of starvation or exposure or who knew what other danger that lurked in that god-forsaken neighborhood. Jack would be devastated. He would blame himself for leaving Polly alone instead of hiding with her.

Please, Lord. Not that.

His ponderings gave Howard the beginnings of a plan. He would go to the police precinct in Jack's neighborhood today and find out what they knew. He wished he could leap from the bed and get started, but he needed to talk to Addy first. The room was growing lighter, and he could read the dial on his alarm clock. Nearly six-thirty. Still too early to awaken her. He chose another string of worry—his finances—and began to unravel that one, as well.

If he started going to work an hour earlier each day, and stayed an hour or so later in the evening, he could add more billable hours and earn more money. He would hate to bring work home in the evenings, but that was a possibility, too. Perhaps he could work at home in the evenings when Adelaide attended her suffrage meetings. No matter what, he made up his mind not to say anything to her about his financial worries. He never wanted her to think that he was unable to provide for her.

Then there was his worry about what to do with Jack if they didn't find his family. Howard had shared his concern with his dad, but hadn't found a solution. They couldn't return Jack to Children's Aid. He would surely run away again and end up living on the streets. Was it the best answer for everyone if Howard and Addy adopted him? Howard couldn't make that decision without talking it over with her, and he didn't know how to go about it. She wasn't ready to become a mother, even if she did have a heart as big as the world.

Howard looked over at his sleeping wife and thought his heart would burst with love. And that brought another pressing worry to mind—what should he buy Addy for Christmas?

Howard was still pondering that question when she finally woke up. They went downstairs in their robes and slippers to fix breakfast for themselves and found Jack already awake and dressed. He looked as though he'd been awake for a long time.

"Can we go look for Polly, now?"

"Let's eat breakfast, first. Mrs. Forsythe and I haven't discussed our plans for the day yet." Jack sighed and slumped in his chair.

"What are our plans?" Addy asked when they returned to their bedroom again. She had opened the wardrobe doors to choose what to wear.

"I've decided to go to the police station in Jack's old neighborhood and see if they have any record of finding Polly."

"That's a great idea!"

"But I think you and Jack should stay home and let me go to the police station by myself."

She turned to look at him with a clothes hanger in her hand. "Why? I thought we were doing this search together."

"Jack's old neighborhood is a rough one, so I'm sure the police station isn't the kind of place you should experience."

The little frown on her face told Howard she was digging in to oppose him. He was right. "I've been to that neighborhood before. I know what it's like. It's not going to shock me."

He decided to be honest with her. "Addy, I'm worried that Polly might have died."

She gripped his arm. "Howard, no!"

"She's a three-year-old child, left on her own in cold weather without food or shelter. I don't think Jack should hear it from the police if she has died. We'll need to find a gentler way to break the news to him."

"You're right. But I'm still going with you. We're doing this together, Howard. And since we can't leave Jack here all alone, he'll have to come, too. He and I will stay in the carriage while you go inside the police station."

He pulled her close and kissed her. "You know, for a beautiful, spoiled heiress, you're a very courageous woman." She gave him a playful swat.

Once again, Howard rented a horse and carriage for the day, and they set off across town to Jack's neighborhood. Jack begged to come inside the police station, and Howard had a hard time convincing him to stay behind. He pulled the boy aside and whispered, "I don't want Mrs. Forsythe to see some of the brutal sights inside the station. And I don't want to leave her all alone out here. Can you stay outside and keep watch for me? You know this neighborhood better than the driver does."

Jack reluctantly agreed, and Howard went inside, bracing himself for tragic news. The station was noisy and chaotic, forcing Howard to wait several minutes before someone attended to him. A raggedy man smelling strongly of alcohol lay across the only three chairs in the waiting area, snoring loudly. A stream of vile cursing flowed from the rear of the station, coming from what Howard presumed were the jail cells. He was glad Addy had stayed outside.

The disheveled cop who finally approached Howard looked in no mood to be polite. To work in a neighborhood like this, cops probably had to be rough characters themselves. "Whadda ya need?" he barked.

Howard slid one of his business cards across the splintery admitting desk. "My name is Howard Forsythe, and I'm searching for a missing child. She's from one of the tenements in this neighborhood. I'm hoping you can help me."

"Are ya kiddin' me? Have you seen how many runaway urchins live in the streets around here? They disappear like roaches when they see a cop coming."

"The child I'm looking for is a three-year-old girl, not a runaway."

The cop seemed to weigh something as he gazed at Howard's card. Then he exhaled. "Ya better come inside and give me the details." He motioned for Howard to follow him farther into the station and take a seat in front of his lopsided desk.

"This search might be as simple as looking through your records," Howard began. "The child's name is Polly Thomas and she disappeared on October twenty-sixth." He laid out every detail he knew, and the officer finally rose to fetch the record file for the month of October.

The handwritten reports were stained and crumpled, but the cop eventually found the report of the police entering Jack's apartment with the building superintendent, removing Mrs. Thomas's dead body, and later finding a small boy hidden inside a cupboard. "It says the kid bit one of the officers when he tried to restrain him."

Howard could well imagine.

"It says they searched the place, looking for any information about the kid's relatives, since he wouldn't cooperate, but found nothing. None of the neighbors seemed willing or able to talk to us. The building superintendent was no help, either. Said he hadn't seen the father in a while, so they removed the dead woman's body and wrestled the kid off to Children's Aid."

"That sounds about right. But what they couldn't have known is that Jack's three-year-old sister was also hiding somewhere."

"Criminy!"

"Can you look to see if she was found later that day or maybe within the next two or three days?"

The cop's brow wrinkled with concern as he shuffled

through the disorganized pages. Howard whispered a silent prayer as minutes passed and the cop squinted at the hand-written reports.

"Here! This might be it!" He looked up briefly and ran his fingers through his hair, which explained its disheveled state. "It says a very young child was seen wandering the streets all alone, looking dazed. That's not unusual except that she was much younger than most street urchins. And she didn't run off when our patrolman approached her." He turned the page over and read more before looking up again. "Hey! You can talk to the guy who found her. O'Malley's here today." He scrambled to his feet and disappeared into the back, calling O'Malley's name. Howard's heart leaped with excitement, even as he tried not to raise his hopes too high.

Officer O'Malley was a burly fellow who looked as though he could lift the desk with one hand. He seemed young, barely eighteen or nineteen years old, and spoke with an accent, which Howard guessed to be Irish.

"Ah, I remember the little gal. I don't think I'm likely to be forgetting her for a good long while. She was walking down the middle of the street, she was, looking like she was in a daze. Muddy, and soaking wet. Cold as ice. She felt like skin and bones when I picked her up. I hurried back to the station with her to warm her up, and I gave her my sandwich. She was an odd little one. Never seen the likes of her. She never cried or said a word in all that time. Mind you, we all tried our best, but we couldn't get her to tell us who she was or where she lived, so we kept her here overnight, waiting for a missing person's report. It never came. We even went back to where I found her, asking if anyone knew her, but no one did."

Howard could barely contain his excitement. "That sounds like it could be her! Where is she now? What happened to her?"

"When we were convinced that no one was looking for her, we had no choice but to take her to an orphans' home."

Howard closed his eyes in relief. Polly was alive! The police knew where she was. Jack could be reunited with his sister. Their prayers had been answered. He rose to his feet, eager to leave right away. "Which orphanage?"

O'Malley winced. The pained look on his young face made Howard's stomach turn.

"Tell me."

"There was something not quite right about her, you see. She wouldn't talk, even though she was surely not a babe, and old enough to talk. She seemed half wild. Made noises like an animal. The sergeant told us we'd better take her to that home for the insane and feebleminded."

"Oh, no." A new fear arose in Howard's heart. "Not the insane asylum on Blackwell's Island?"

"That place closed down five or six years ago," the first cop said. "All because of that lady reporter. What was her name?"

"You mean Nellie Bly?" Howard asked.

"Yeah. That's the one."

Howard knew all about Nellie Bly. A young journalist for the *New York World*, she had pretended to be insane and gotten herself committed to the New York Lunatic Asylum on Blackwell's Island. Her report on the conditions there shocked the city. She had said that a few days in the asylum could drive even the sanest people insane. "So where is Polly?"

"They took her to Randall's Island."

The news made Howard's stomach sink even further. Along with Blackwell's Island and Wards Island, Randall's Island was a place of last resort for New York's poorest and most damaged residents. He thanked the officers for their help and hurried outside to tell Addy and Jack the news. "I think I may know where she is. The police found a little girl matching Polly's description wandering in the street and took her to an orphans' home."

Jack gave a cry of joy. "You found her?"

Addy gripped Howard's arm. "Where? Which orphanage?"

He lowered his voice, hoping Jack wouldn't hear or understand. "It's a terrible place, Addy. I need to take you and Jack home first, and—"

"Nothing doing. We're going there together."

"Addy, they house insane people there."

"I'm coming with you!" Jack cried. "I know what Polly looks like! And she knows me!"

"He's right, Howard."

"All right, I'll take Jack with me, but you should—"

"Stop arguing. We're both coming with you."

Getting to Randall's Island, located between the Harlem and East Rivers, proved to be a long and frustrating journey. Howard paid off the carriage driver and let him leave as they waited to take a ferry to the island, knowing it might take a long time to locate Polly within the maze of public institutions. While onboard, Jack wandered off to explore the ferry, giving Howard a chance to tell Addy what he knew about Randall's Island. "That unfortunate island has become a dumping ground for all the so-called 'undesirable' people no one knows what to do with."

"Then why in the world did they take a three-year-old child there?"

Howard glanced over at Jack, standing by the rail, and

lowered his voice. "The police said the same thing everyone else has been saying about Polly. There's something strange about her. And she wouldn't talk."

"Jack has been saying that she'll only talk to him."

"Well, let's hope she's still there. And that she's all right."

They approached the largest building after landing, and endured an interminable wait before speaking with someone in charge. Even Addy's connection to the Stanhope Foundation didn't seem to make a difference. The man who finally approached them seemed harried and unapologetic. "We're looking for a missing child," Howard said, handing him his card. "We were told by the police that she was brought here."

"Brought where? This is a big place." He put the card into his pocket without looking at it. "There's a poor house, the House of Refuge for young delinquents, a homeopathic hospital, an asylum for hopeless drunkards, another one for idiots, and the city's asylum for the insane."

Howard exhaled, trying not to imagine a frightened three-year-old in any of those places. "Where would I most likely find a child about three years old, without a name or any identification? She doesn't talk." He wanted to add that the police had described Polly as "wild," but he didn't want to say it in front of Jack.

"Try the Idiot Asylum. They take children." Addy drew a sharp breath at his words. Howard quickly gripped Jack's shoulders to keep him from leaping to Polly's defense, recalling how he'd attacked another boy for calling her feebleminded.

"Thank you. Can you direct us there?"

The man gave them directions, and as they made their way to the building, Howard tried to warn Jack and Addy that what they were about to witness might be very difficult to see. And he was right. The entrance lobby alone made Howard shudder. It smelled foul and echoed with the distant sound of moans and cries. After another long delay, they finally were escorted to the asylum director's office. A grumpy-looking, gray-haired woman with the attitude and defensive posture of a prison guard met them. "The director doesn't work on Saturdays," she told them. "I'm his assistant. What do you need?" She showed no compassion as Howard told her Polly's story. She began shaking her head before he'd even finished. "You may as well make an appointment and come back another day. It would take hours to look through all our records."

"You would only need to go back to the end of October," Addy said. "Barely two months ago."

"We're very short-handed at the moment." The woman

remained standing beside the director's desk, arms crossed, making no move to begin the search.

Howard battled not to lose his temper. They were so close to finding Polly, and he wanted to shake this woman. "How can we get the process started?" he asked.

"We're willing to help any way we can," Addy added. "We'll help you search the records if—"

"Our records are private. And this isn't my office. I would need authorization."

Howard knew they could easily go inside and search for Polly among the patients, but clearly, the woman had no intention of letting them proceed any further. He guessed that because of Nellie Bly's exposé, the administrators didn't want outsiders and reporters to see the asylum's living conditions. He turned to Jack to see how the boy was handling this latest disappointment—but he was gone.

"Where's Jack?" he asked Addy.

She shook her head as she glanced all around. "I-I don't know. He was here a moment ago." She looked up at him, and Howard could tell she was trying not to smile. "But I can guess where he is. He did this once before at one of the orphanages we visited."

"Let's go." Howard grabbed Addy's hand and hurried from the office without waiting for permission.

"Sir! Ma'am! Where are you going? Wait!"

Howard turned to shout over his shoulder. "The boy is looking for his sister. If she's here, he'll find her!"

"But you can't just—"

"It's the simplest way." Ignoring her protests, Howard and Addy hurried through room after room on the first floor, calling Jack's name. Howard thought he'd been prepared for what they might witness, but conditions in the asylum were more shocking than he could have imagined. Vulnerable human beings of all ages and disabilities, society's most helpless people, were being forced to live in appalling conditions simply because they were poor and disabled. He didn't know if the director's assistant was still chasing them or if she was summoning the guards. He didn't care.

"Jack! Jack, where are you?" he continued to call out. They came to a sunroom at the rear of the building that might have been a pleasant room on a warmer, sunnier day. Today it was as chilly and bleak on the inside as outside. Howard had taken one step into the room when Addy stopped him.

"Howard, look!"

Jack stood on the other side of the room, clutching a frail wisp of a girl in his embrace. He was weeping and saying "Polly! Polly!" over and over as he rocked her. The sound of his cries, whether from joy or sorrow or both, echoed off the glass windows and tiled floor. Polly made a keening sound, like a wounded animal, as she clung to him. Would she ever be the same after living in a place like this for nearly two months? The other patients had stopped what they were doing to stare.

Howard started forward, but Addy stopped him again. "Wait. Give them a minute." She was using her handkerchief to wipe her tears. He pulled out his to wipe his own. He couldn't remember a more poignant, fulfilling moment in his life.

Then he heard footsteps behind him and turned to see that the assistant director had caught up with them. She was breathing hard. "What are you doing? You can't just go running through here! I've called for the orderlies to escort you out!"

Howard pointed to the two children, his emotions so intense he could barely speak. "That little girl is Polly Thomas, Jack's sister. We're going to take her home with us."

"You can't do that. There's paperwork that must be filled out. We'll need proof that she belongs with you."

"Look at her with her brother. Do you need any more proof than that?"

"And what is your relationship to these children?"

"Children's Aid has placed Jack in our care. We've been helping him search for his sister. Orphaned siblings aren't supposed to be separated, but unfortunately, these two were. We've spent a great deal of time and effort trying to find Polly, and now she's coming home with us. Today."

Howard's calm insistence seemed to surprise the woman. She sputtered for a reply. But the admiring look that Addy gave him made all Howard's time and expense worthwhile. He'd become her hero. She squeezed his hand before releasing it to walk over to Jack and Polly. Howard watched his wife kneel to talk to the children, ignoring the assistant director's final, sputtering protests. Jack had released Polly, and was gesturing as if telling Polly who Addy was and how they'd been searching for her. Polly smiled, then clung to Jack again, as if determined to never let go. Howard swiped his tears and repeated what he'd already told the woman. "Polly Thomas is coming home with us today. If there's any paperwork, you'd better do it quickly."

A few minutes later, Addy stood and walked back to Howard, beckoning for the children to follow her. "Howard, I don't think Polly is feebleminded," she whispered. "I think she's deaf!"

The asylum had discarded the clothing Polly had arrived in, so Howard carried her outside to the ferry landing in the rough gray gown that all the inmates wore. It was much too large for her, and nearly threadbare, so he swaddled her in his own coat as they recrossed the river by ferry, then flagged down a carriage for the journey home.

Jack sat on the floor in the upstairs bathroom, refusing to leave Polly's side while Addy bathed her in the tub and washed her hair. The fragrant aroma of rose-scented bath salts filled the air. When Polly was dry and wrapped in one of Addy's bathrobes, they all went down to the kitchen and raided the larder and icebox, spreading the food Mrs. Gleason had left for them on the kitchen table. All four of them dove into the celebration feast, with Jack and Polly sharing the same kitchen chair. The silence between the children as they communicated with their eyes and hands seemed strange, yet the joy and love they shared were obvious. Howard couldn't stop smiling.

"You're right," he told Addy. "I can tell by the alert intelligence in Polly's eyes that she isn't feebleminded." As a test, he dropped a copper pot on the kitchen floor behind her back, but she never flinched or turned toward the noise.

"I can't imagine the suffering those two children have endured in their short lives," Addy said when they were alone in bed, later. Jack and Polly had insisted on sleeping in the little maid's room near the kitchen, refusing to be separated again. Howard didn't blame them.

"And they're just two of many thousands of children in this city with tragic stories," he replied.

"I'm going to do something about it. At least, I'm going to try," Addy said. Howard held her close, loving her for her courage and her tender heart.

PART 3

THE CANDLE OF JOY

Joy to the world, the Lord is come!
Let earth receive her King!
ISAAC WATTS, "Joy to the World"

You turned my wailing into dancing;
you removed my sackcloth and clothed me with joy.

PSALM 30:11

CHAPTER 9

SUNDAY, DECEMBER 15

Jack and Polly sat on the same chair as if glued to each other as they ate breakfast. Polly's wide blue eyes, which were so much like Jack's, had lost most of the stark terror Howard had seen in them yesterday. Her wispy brown hair, matted and tangled before last night's bath, reminded him of dandelion fluff. She seemed pale and frail, like a puff of smoke that might vanish in the wind.

"Maybe we should stay home from church today to give Polly a chance to recover a bit more," Howard suggested. Jack's instant outrage surprised him.

"No! We gotta go! We gotta light another candle and pray for Papa!"

"But Polly doesn't have any clothes to wear, or a warm coat," Howard said.

"It doesn't matter! We gotta go! She can wear my coat. Polly told me that she wants to go!"

Howard had no idea how Jack knew his sister's wishes. The strange, silent communication between them remained a mystery. He turned to Addy, who shrugged and said, "I guess we're going."

"If we hurry and get there early," Howard said, "maybe my mother can find something for Polly to wear from the charity box." They dressed her in one of Jack's shirts and a pair of his trousers, rolling up the cuffs. Addy swaddled Polly in her warmest shawl, and Howard carried her in his arms. He hailed a carriage for the ride to church rather than subjecting the tiny girl to a tedious trolley ride. Howard's mother was washing the breakfast dishes when the four of them trailed through the kitchen door of the parsonage. Howard couldn't help grinning. "Mom, meet Jack's sister, Polly."

His mother was so overcome with emotion she swayed in place. "Oh, my goodness! You found her! Oh, heavens be praised! And isn't she a little darling!"

"Is Dad still here?"

She nodded as she stared at Polly with tears in her eyes. Howard called to his father, who hurried in from the front room a moment later.

"What's going on? Who—? Oh, my. You found her, then." He reached to gently caress Polly's hair as if to see if she was real.

"The police found her wandering the streets nearly two months ago." He lowered his voice, even though he knew she couldn't hear him. "She's been living in the Idiot Asylum on Randall's Island since the end of October."

"Oh, no . . . no," his mother breathed.

"Polly is deaf, Mom. And as you can see, she needs clothes." He set the girl on the floor beside her brother. His father crouched down to address the children.

"I'll tell you what, Jack. You and your sister can light all three Advent candles for the service today. Would you like that?"

Jack beamed as he nodded in reply. "What candle is it this week?"

"It's joy," Reverend Forsythe replied. "It's the candle of joy."

"I need to leave for work earlier than usual all this week," Howard told Addy on Monday morning. "And I'm sorry to say I'll be home a little later every night, too. Don't wait for me to eat dinner with you. Go ahead and eat with the children."

The news wasn't what Addy wanted to hear. She remembered the long days her father had spent at work, making him a stranger to his family. He'd died at only forty-six years of age. "Why the extra hours?" she asked as she watched him button his overcoat.

"There are a few things I need to wrap up before the end of the year."

Howard hadn't met her gaze when he'd told her the news. She still didn't know him well enough to guess his thoughts or motives. She didn't like it that they would have less time to spend together. They needed to talk about Polly and Jack, and how they could go about finding their father, not to mention what would become of the children if their father didn't return home.

"I'll give Jack and Polly their dinner, but I'll wait to eat mine with you," she said. She kissed him goodbye.

Addy was in the kitchen with the children when Mrs. Gleason arrived. The cook took one look at Jack's beaming face as he stood holding Polly's hand and she bent to pull both children into her arms. "Oh, Jackie-boy! You found her! I'm so very, very happy for you!" She finally released them to wipe her tears and looked Polly over from head to toe. "Aren't you a beautiful child!" Polly smiled up at Mrs. Gleason as if she'd known her all her life.

"I can't believe you found her," Susannah said, wiping her tears. "Where was she?"

Addy didn't want to describe the horrible asylum where Polly had been living. She paused, then said, "The police in the children's old neighborhood were able to tell us where she'd been taken. We've also learned that Polly is deaf."

"Oh, bless your little heart, child," Mrs. Gleason said, stroking Polly's hair. "God bless your little heart."

Addy swallowed. "As you can see, she's going to need some new clothes. The dress she's wearing came from the church's charity bin. You'll come shopping with me, won't you, Susannah?"

"Oh, yes, ma'am. I would be happy to."

"I was thinking we would go tomorrow to give Polly more time to adjust. She still seems shaky and fearful at times, even with Jack by her side. Attending church yesterday tired her out, and she fell asleep on Howard's lap on the ride home."

"She looks like she could do with a few good meals, too,"

Mrs. Gleason said. "I'll set about fattening her up, don't you worry."

The following day, Addy walked to the trolley stop with Susannah and the children for the trip to Dixon's Department Store. They had bundled Polly up in one of Addy's jackets, rolling up the sleeves. Susannah carried the girl since the bulky coat hung nearly to Polly's ankles. Polly scrambled onto Jack's lap during the ride, gazing out the window in wonder. Addy decided to use the time on their trolley ride to coach Susannah. "Remember, now. Pay close attention to what the salesclerk says and does so we can practice again when we get home. You can easily do her job, Susannah. You're a bright girl."

"I've been doing what you said and walking with a book on my head at home."

"Good."

"And smiling in the mirror, too. But Auntie caught me and said I was being vain. I tried to explain what you'd told me to do, but I'm not sure she believed me."

Addy hid a smile, imagining the no-nonsense Mrs. Gleason's reaction when she saw Susannah preening. "I'll explain it to her, if it will help. But tell me, what have you learned from these exercises?"

Susannah shrugged. "I don't know. I guess standing tall does make me feel different. Like I don't need to hide."

"Good. You'll be ready to apply for a job before you know it."

"What about my hands?" she asked, holding them out. "They're so red and chapped from scrubbing."

"Hm. I'll ask Mrs. Gleason if we can use milder soap."

As they neared their trolley stop, Jack nudged Polly to her feet to prepare to get off. He'd only taken this route once before, so Addy was surprised he remembered. He was a very perceptive little boy.

With only a week remaining until Christmas Eve, the streets and sidewalks and stores were busier and more crowded than usual. Again, Susannah carried Polly so she could see better, and to avoid being crushed. The little girl gazed at the unfamiliar sights and sounds with a mixture of wonder and fear. The contrast between where she was now and where she'd been for the first three years of her life couldn't have been sharper. Jack surprised Addy again when he remembered which store window had a display of toys, and led them straight to it. He studied his sister's face, not the toys, as she gazed at dollhouses and hobbyhorses, a miniature porcelain tea set, and a baby doll in a little cradle. There was a toy locomotive on an oval track, toy horses pulling a firemen's hook and ladder wagon, and a doll-size range like the one in their kitchen with tiny pots and pans. Addy let the children look for as long as they liked, promising herself that she would come back alone and choose Christmas presents for them. And something for Susannah and Mrs. Gleason, too.

Inside, a different young clerk waited on them in Dixon's girls' department. After deliberating and trying on a variety of items, they purchased two dresses for Polly, a pinafore, woolen stockings, a flannel nightgown, undergarments, button-up leather shoes, and a warm overcoat. At times, Polly clung to Jack, clearly frightened by so many strangers and such unusual surroundings. Each time, he was able to soothe her and continue shopping. Addy added the purchases to Howard's account as he had insisted.

"I thought our salesclerk did an excellent job," Addy said on the way home. "Tell me what you learned, Susannah."

"I noticed that she was watching us all the time, paying close attention."

"Yes, and she anticipated our needs."

"When she saw that we liked something, or didn't like it, or it was the wrong size, she acted right away."

"Very good. Anything else?"

"She was right there when we needed her, but sometimes

she stood back and stayed out of our way so we could talk amongst ourselves."

"Yes, she was very good about that. So. Do you think you could do her job?"

Susannah gave a slow, shy smile that lit up her pretty face. "I think I could."

"I do, too." Addy was excited and happy for this young girl who was daring to dream of a better life. Such an opportunity should be available to every young woman. If only Addy could figure out a way to make it possible.

Once again, Jack knew where to get off to change trolley lines, and which trolley number to wait for to take them home. Addy made a note to mention it to Howard, and ask how Jack's keen memory might be put to good use.

Mrs. Gleason had cookies waiting for the children when they returned home. They raced down the stairs without waiting to remove their coats, drawn by the heavenly aroma of cinnamon. Addy took Susannah upstairs to play at being a salesclerk again. "Excellent! You're getting the hang of it," Addy said after they practiced. "Now, please take your hairpins out and let your hair down. I want you to brush it out." She held out her engraved silver hairbrush.

"I-I couldn't! Your brush is much too fancy for someone like me."

"Nonsense. It's just a brush." Addy had only recently learned how to arrange her own hair without the help of a ladies' maid, but she made Susannah sit down at her dressing table and shared what she'd learned with her. Perhaps a new set of hair combs would make a good Christmas present for her. The girl was very pretty, with a fresh, wholesome innocence about her. "See? Doesn't your hair look better when it's not pulled back so tightly?" Addy asked when they'd finished experimenting.

Susannah blushed at her reflection. "I look like one of those Gibson girls."

"Exactly. You're a very pretty girl, Susannah. And here, I want to give you this jar of facial cream and bar of soap—"

"Oh, I couldn't!"

"I think the soap you're using to wash your face is much too harsh. It's burning your skin."

"We only ever had homemade soap on the farm."

"I think you'll find this is much better for your skin. And you can probably buy something like it at a five-and-dime store when this runs out."

Later, downstairs in the parlor, Addy watched Susannah walk with a book balanced on her head, happy to see the progress she'd made. Jack and Polly came upstairs and wanted to walk with books on their heads too, so it became a game that produced much laughter and giggles. Mrs. Gleason smiled as she watched from the top of the kitchen steps. Addy wished Howard could be here to see this. His extended working hours were causing him to miss so much.

"Thank you for everything you're doing for my niece," Mrs. Gleason whispered to Addy, later. "You've been so good to us, Mrs. Forsythe."

"I'm happy to do it. I don't know how I ever would have managed these past few weeks without you and Susannah."

In all the excitement of finding Polly, Addy hadn't had time to get nervous about hosting fifteen of her wealthy friends in her home for tea. But on the day before the event, she began to fret. She remained in the kitchen after breakfast so she could talk with Mrs. Gleason, hoping the cook had some advice to help settle her nerves. The winter morning was mild for mid-December, and Susannah had taken the children outside to play in the slushy snow.

"May I watch you work?" Addy asked. "I would still like to learn how to cook a few simple things."

Mrs. Gleason smiled as she set a sack of flour on the table. "What I have planned for your friends will be anything but simple. I'm making a Lady Baltimore cake, some fancy pastries with dates and figs, and some macarons. I've been told by other cooks I know that everyone is serving little club sandwiches these days instead of cheese and cress."

"Everything sounds delicious. May I help? It's the only way I'll ever learn."

"Of course. I'll fetch you an apron and put you to work."

Addy chopped nuts and dates, creamed butter, and beat egg whites with a whisk until her arm ached. "May I ask you a question, Mrs. Gleason?" she said when she paused to rest her arm. "Jack prayed so hard to find Polly, and God answered his prayers. Now he's praying that his father will come home safely but . . . what if he doesn't return? What will we tell Jack? I would hate to see him lose his innocent faith."

"Well, now that's one of those harder questions to answer, isn't it? Just like there are dishes you can cook up in a jiffy and ones that take more time and care. I've prayed some pretty big prayers over the years that seemed to go unanswered. And if I wasn't careful, I could start to believe that God didn't love me because He didn't give me what I'd asked for. I had to learn that my faith shouldn't depend on whether or not God answers my prayers exactly the way I want Him to."

"That's a lesson I'm still struggling to learn. How can we explain it to a little child?"

She paused from her work and met Addy's gaze. "I don't know. But I do know we can trust the Almighty. If Mr. Thomas doesn't return, then God must have a better plan for those lovely children."

Addy hesitated before asking the question she hadn't been able to push aside. "Do you think His plan is for Howard and me to adopt them? Do you think that's why He arranged for Jack to land on our doorstep?"

Mrs. Gleason sighed and wiped her hands on her apron. "I don't think it's as simple as that, dear. But I do know He has a plan for them. Right now, you've played a huge part by helping them find each other. If God asks more from you and Mr. Forsythe, He'll make it clear to you when the time is right."

There was a commotion at the back door and a rush of cold air as Susannah and the children came inside, laughing and stomping snow from their feet. Their cheeks were pink from the cold and each of them carried an armload of evergreen branches. The scent of pine wafted into the kitchen.

"Goodness! What's all this?" Addy asked.

"I thought we could decorate your parlor, ma'am. For your tea party tomorrow." She dropped her load in the back hallway and directed the children to do the same. They had filled the coal scuttle with pine cones and vines of red bittersweet berries.

"I helped," Jack said. "Susannah said I was a big help, right?"

"I'm sure you were, Jackie-boy. Just look at that load you're carrying." Mrs. Gleason brushed pine needles from his hair, then pulled a handkerchief from her apron pocket and wiped Polly's runny nose. The tender gestures came so naturally to her, but not to Addy. Would she even make a good mother for these children if that's what God asked? She would have so much to learn about motherhood, along with learning to cook and to clean, and she didn't feel ready for such an important task. Was she selfish to want more time alone with her new husband?

They spread the branches on newspaper so they could dry, then carried them upstairs after lunch. Susannah showed amazing artistry in the way she draped the parlor's mantel with evergreens, pine cones, and bittersweet berries. She festooned the windowsills with more greenery and wrapped some of it around the stair rail leading to the second floor. She filled a silver bowl with more greenery and berries, and arranged it as a centerpiece for the dining room table, flanked by Addy's silver candlesticks. By the time she finished, the aroma of pine filled the entire house. She had ironed Addy's best linen tablecloth for tomorrow and added all the extensions to the table. Jack and Polly helped her polish the silver tea service.

"Everything looks beautiful!" Addy said when they'd finished. "It looks and smells like Christmas in here. I can't wait for Howard to see it."

He arrived home very late and seemed preoccupied, as if his mind was still on his work. "It smells wonderful in here," he said as he hung his hat and overcoat on the hall tree. Addy took his hand and pulled him into the parlor, eager to show him the town house's transformation. "Wow! Good thing you met me at the door or I would think I was in the wrong place! Are these decorations for your tea tomorrow?"

"Yes. Susannah came up with the idea and then did this all on her own. I simply stood back and watched."

"It looks amazing."

"I did help Mrs. Gleason prepare some of the food for the tea, though. She's showing me how to do a few simple things in the kitchen. You'll be so proud of me when I can cook dinner for us, someday."

He stroked her cheek. "Even if you cooked a feast, I couldn't possibly be more proud of you than I already am."

She smiled at his praise. "We'll have to eat in the kitchen

tonight, since Susannah already prepared the dining room for the tea."

"I don't mind. I like our cozy little kitchen. Give me a minute to wash up and I'll meet you down there." Addy started to leave but he held onto her hand, stopping her. "It's so quiet. Where are Jack and Polly?"

"They're in bed. It's very late. They played outside in the snow for the longest time, and helped Susannah with all these branches. They were worn out." Howard pulled her into his embrace.

"Addy, I'm sorry I was so late. I hope you weren't worried."

"I was. A little. But it doesn't matter. You're here, now." She hurried downstairs where the kitchen table already was set for the two of them. She pulled the food Mrs. Gleason had prepared from the warming oven, and it did feel strange to eat a fine, pork roast dinner in the kitchen. This would have been the servants' table in the mansion where she grew up. She sometimes forgot that Howard had grown up in a cozy parsonage and probably felt more at home eating in the kitchen beside the warm range than in a formal dining room. When they were seated with their food in front of them, she looked closer at his handsome face and noticed worry lines that hadn't been there before, and dark circles beneath his eyes. She reached across the table to stroke his brow. "Are you feeling all right, Howard? Is anything wrong?"

"I'm just tired. We'll get through this busy patch at work in a few more weeks—"

"Weeks?"

"I'm sorry."

They finished dinner and went to bed not long afterwards. Howard fell asleep right away. Once again, he had set his alarm clock to leave the house early. It took Addy much longer to fall asleep as she checked off mental lists of preparations for her tea and silently rehearsed what she wanted to tell her friends about the fight for women's suffrage. She wondered what their reactions would be to her new way of life. She hoped they wouldn't be condescending. Or worse, pitying. Addy doubted if she could control her temper if anyone dared to pity her. She was the wealthiest woman in the world!

She was waiting by the front door to greet her guests the following afternoon with Susannah at her side to take the guests' coats. The maid looked impressive in a dark uniform and frilly white apron, starched to a crisp stiffness. One by one, her friends entered and gazed around the town house. Addy could tell by their expressions that they were surprised and a little impressed.

"What a charming home," her friend Felicity said.

"Yes, it's lovely," another guest said. "I could easily live here."

Addy thought she understood what her friend meant. Addy's seventy-five-room mansion had been so cold and echoing that she had always felt most at home in the cozy morning room, which was as snug and cheerful as this parlor.

Her guests raved about the food, as Addy knew they would. "You must tell me which bakery you used," one of them begged.

"Our cook, Mrs. Gleason, made everything, including the Lady Baltimore cake."

"She didn't!"

"Lucky you!"

"I helped her make the date and fig bars. She's teaching me to cook and I'm enjoying it very much." For a moment, the room fell still, as if her words had shocked them into silence. Addy smiled and gestured to the table. "Please, help yourselves to more."

She gave her guests plenty of time to chat and gossip about other things while they ate and sipped their tea, then signaled to Susannah to bring Jack and Polly upstairs to be introduced. The children wore their Sunday best, and Susannah had braided Polly's wispy hair into pigtails, tied with red satin ribbons. Addy heard murmurs of "how sweet" and "so adorable." She rose to stand beside them, resting her hands on Jack's shoulders so he wouldn't fidget or bolt. "Friends, I would like you to meet my special guests, Polly and Jack Thomas. They've been staying with Howard and me while we wait for their father to return from overseas. Sadly, their mother died last October. At first, the children were separated and sent to two different orphanages before Howard and I were able to reunite them.

"Do you have any idea how many orphans' homes there are in this city? Here's a partial list of some of the ones the Stanhope Charitable Foundation supports." Addy unfurled the list her mother had given her and held it up. "Many of the children in these orphanages aren't orphans at all. Much too often, their mothers have become so impoverished that they're unable to take care of their little ones. One infant arrived at the orphanage with this note pinned to his clothing:

'I leave my little son in your hands with the hope that he will be lovingly cared for here. I would never leave my child if it was possible for me to make a respectable living for the two of us, but it is not. Please take care of my little boy. His name is Joseph.'"

Once again, the room had grown very still. "That's a tragedy, don't you think? Joseph had to be separated from his mother and sent to an institution because she couldn't make 'a respectable living.' And it is mothers like little Joseph's who the suffrage movement is trying to help. I know many of you probably see the movement as a bunch of angry women with placards, demanding the right to vote. But we're trying to accomplish so much more than that, and we need to be heard in order to do it. If we could vote, we could fight for women to have better access to higher education and professional degrees. We would ask that the jobs available to women offered better wages, so mothers like Joseph's could support their families. We would make sure that women were paid the same wages as men, not less, for doing the same work.

"The start of this new century should be a time of new beginnings for women. Yes, we are still wives and mothers. But we want to be respected as equal members of society, with an equal right to express our opinions through voting."

Addy paused to survey her friends' reactions and was pleased that they seemed to be listening. "I'll get off my soapbox, now," she said with a smile. "But if you're interested, I would love to talk more about the suffrage movement with you. I'm happy to answer your questions, and I hope you will join me at one of our meetings so you can hear what our very gifted speakers have to say." She nodded to Susannah, signaling that the children could leave, and held up the list of orphanages again. "If nothing else, would you consider contributing to one of these orphanages so they can buy new clothing and Christmas presents for the children? A child's winter coat costs two dollars and forty-five cents in the Sears, Roebuck catalogue. I recently bought a new hat that could have clothed several orphans at that price. I know you are all good-hearted women. I would love to have you join me in my work."

When the last guest left, Addy wanted to cheer in triumph. She raced down to the kitchen to thank Susannah and Mrs. Gleason and tell them the good news. "The tea was a wonderful success, thanks to you. I think my friends came here prepared to pity me, but judging by their reactions, they seemed surprised and impressed. They were listening, truly listening, when I shared about the women and children who need our help. Three of my friends asked if they could go to the next suffrage meeting with me."

"That's wonderful news, dear!"

"It's a start, at least. And I couldn't have done it without both of you. Thank you, thank you!"

Addy could hardly wait for Howard to come home so

she could celebrate the news of her success with him. But her enthusiasm waned as the hour grew later and later. The children were put to bed. Mrs. Gleason's lovely roast chicken began to shrivel and dry out in the warming oven. When he finally arrived, she told him about the tea as they ate together at the kitchen table, but her excitement had dimmed. "I saved you a piece of Lady Baltimore cake. You must try it. Mrs. Gleason and Susannah are godsends."

"It sounds like a rousing success, darling. Congratulations." Howard had listened with interest, but she noticed him trying to stifle his yawns. His blue eyes lacked their usual sparkle.

"You look exhausted, Howard. You've been getting up in the dark and coming home in the dark. I believe that's what's called 'burning the candle at both ends.'"

He reached for her hand. "I'm sorry that I've been so busy. I'll make it up to you, I promise. We'll get a Christmas tree this weekend and the children can help us decorate it."

"I'm excited about our first Christmas together. But to be honest, I'm very worried about how the children will react if their father doesn't return home."

"I know. I'm worried, too."

"If it's all right with you, I would like to buy presents for Jack and Polly, and a little something special for Susannah and Mrs. Gleason to thank them for all their help."

"Of course." He looked away, but not before Addy saw worry lines crease his forehead and gather around his eyes.

"Go up to bed, Howard. I'll clear away these dishes and join you shortly."

"I can help."

"Another time. Go on."

Addy had spent the long evening brooding and worrying while she'd waited for Howard to come home. Maybe tonight wasn't the best time to talk with him, as tired as he was. But as she put the last of the leftover food in the icebox and carried the dishes to the sink, she decided not to wash them after all. She needed to share her concerns with him tonight. She changed into her nightgown and climbed into bed beside him. But instead of turning out the light, she faced him, taking his hands in hers. "I want to ask you a question, Howard, and I want an honest answer from you."

He looked worried, but he nodded and said, "All right."

She drew a deep breath then exhaled. "Are you working all these extra hours because you're worried about our finances?" When he didn't reply, his silence told her the answer. "Please, be honest with me. Our marriage must be based on trust."

He sighed, looking down at their joined hands. "Well . . ." He sighed again. "Well, we've had a few extra expenses this month that weren't in our budget. But I knew that if I worked a few extra hours this week, I could make up the difference. It's only temporary, I promise."

Tears filled Addy's eyes. "I'm so sorry, Howard. Those extra expenses were my fault. I let Jack stay here without asking you first. Then I bought clothes for him and Polly, and we had to hire all those carriages for our searches—"

"Addy, listen—"

"No, let me finish. We agreed to hire a housekeeper, but I got carried away and hired a cook along with a housekeeper. And then I hosted a tea for my friends and spent even more money that wasn't in our budget. I need to say I'm sorry, Howard. So sorry. You're wearing yourself out with work and worry because of my impulsive decisions."

"I don't see it that way. No one can put a price tag on what it meant to those children to find each other again. We rescued Polly from that terrible asylum! When I think about that place . . . !"

"I know. It was a miracle." Addy let go of his hands to wipe a tear. "But we've created the even bigger problem of what will happen to Polly and Jack after Christmas if their father doesn't come. We've only been married a short time. Is it selfish of me to want some more time alone with you? Just the two of us?"

"If it is, then I'm selfish, too."

"I wish I was better prepared for motherhood, but I'm not. I was raised by nursemaids, and it pains me to admit that Jack and Polly turn to Mrs. Gleason for motherly love and affection, not to me. I wish I could be the wonderful wife and mother that your mother is, but it may take years for me to learn everything."

"Addy, I don't expect you to be like my mother—or anyone else. I want you to be the woman you are. The woman I fell in love with and married. And there's a big difference between getting used to being a parent from the very start of a child's life, and having them thrust upon you when they're three and eight years old. I've been thinking about Jack and Polly a lot, too. I don't think we're the right couple to adopt them. We're newly married and totally unprepared for an instant family."

"But we can't take them back to the orphanage. Jack will run away again. He's done it before. Do you think we could try to find a family willing to adopt them?"

"It might be difficult with Polly being deaf. I've investigated that a bit, too, and learned that the finest schools for deaf children are all boarding schools. And we both know we can't separate the children again."

"I'm so sorry I created this problem in the first place.

I didn't think it through when I took Jack into our home, and now it has gotten too big for me."

"It's because you have a big heart, darling. And I love you for that. We'll figure something out."

"Well, until we do, I've decided that I should pay for all their extra expenses from my inheritance, from now on."

He shook his head, his expression stern. "Addy—"

"But it's only right. Then you wouldn't have to work such long hours."

"You know how I feel about dipping into your inheritance. That money is for your future. If anything should happen to me, I want to make sure you'll be taken care of. I don't want you and any children we may have to end up indigent."

"I understand. You've explained it before. But I need you to listen to my side of it. Please?"

"All right. Go on."

"My grandmother inherited a great deal of money when her husband died, but she gave it all away. Every cent of it. And it brought her great joy to do it. She used her money to build a charitable foundation that has benefited thousands of people over the years. She purchased a boarding house for single mothers like your grandmother. And she invested anonymously in your and your brothers' educations. Remember?"

"How can I forget? I wouldn't be a lawyer if it weren't for her."

"She believed it wasn't right to leave money sitting in a trust fund for some future rainy day when it could be used to change lives today. I want to follow her example, Howard. I want to invest our inheritance in people. And I have an idea for how I would like to go about it."

Howard was no longer frowning. "Go on."

She drew a breath and squared her shoulders. "These past few weeks, I've been training Susannah to be a shop clerk. She dreams of working in a lovely store like Dixon's, someday."

"Susannah? Our maid?"

"Yes. I've been wanting to tell you about it, but we've both been so busy I haven't had a chance. Anyway, she's almost ready to apply for a job."

Howard smiled. "Won't you be losing your housekeeper?"

"Yes, but that's not important. I want to start a school for bright, young girls like her, a place where they can learn skills that will help them get better jobs. Skills like how to operate a typewriting machine and do other office work. There are young women in orphanages all over this city who will never be adopted by a family. And when they become too old to live there and are sent away, they have very little hope of escaping a life of poverty. Listen, it's our inheritance, Howard, not just mine. Let's spend it in a way that shows God's love. Jesus gave up the riches and glory of heaven to become a poor, helpless baby who slept in a borrowed manger. He owned the wealth of the entire universe, but He didn't come to be served but to serve others. Let's invest in helping people. When our money is gone, it's gone. We'll live like everyone else does."

"But I don't want you to ever lack for a single thing."

"I already have everything I will ever need."

He looked away, running his hand through his hair. "This is very hard for me, Addy. It's a husband's job to take care of his wife—"

"I know. But we shouldn't let money be our security. We can trust God for the future, can't we? Hasn't He taken care of us and our families all these years? Even after my father died and Mother and I lost so much, what seemed like a disaster wasn't. We had a chance to start all over again, and in a brand-new way. It was the best thing that could have ever happened because I met you!"

Howard kissed her and held her close. "He has certainly blessed me with a remarkable wife." He kissed her again. "I do like your idea, Addy. And you're right, we can trust God. Just give me some time to think about it, all right? I promise we'll dream about it some more together. But for now, you don't need to spend any of your inheritance. Agreed?"

Addy nodded. Reluctantly. And silently promised herself that she would watch her spending more carefully from now on.

CHAPTER 10

Addy wore an apron over her dress as she stood in front of the kitchen range, gently scrambling eggs in a cast-iron pan. The warmth of the stove heated her cheeks. "You don't want to cook them on the hottest place on the stove," Mrs. Gleason coached. "The secret to good eggs is 'low and slow.' Don't let the fire get too hot and don't cook them too fast."

"Or burn them, right?" Addy chuckled. She had eaten a few of her failed attempts this past week and agreed that scorched eggs tasted terrible.

Mrs. Gleason hovered near her shoulder. "That's perfect! Quickly, now! Slide them onto the plates."

Addy dished the eggs onto two plates and served them to Jack and Polly, who were bouncing on their seats at the kitchen table, eagerly awaiting breakfast. "I can't wait to surprise Howard this weekend," she told Mrs. Gleason. "He's been so busy at work that he's out of the house before I've a chance to make tea and toast."

"Does he like pancakes? I can show you how to make them next week."

"I think he would love that." She smiled at Jack and said, "Remember now, it's a secret. Don't tell Mr. Forsythe that I'm learning to cook."

He shoveled a forkful of eggs into his mouth and said, "We won't."

Addy carried the frying pan to the sink where Susannah was washing dishes, then motioned for her and Mrs. Gleason to follow her into the pantry. She lowered her voice to a whisper. "Would you mind watching the children for me for a little while, Mrs. Gleason? I want to buy a Christmas present for each of the children and I would like Susannah to come with me."

"Not at all. You go ahead, dear, and don't worry about us."

"I know that caring for two children wasn't what you signed up to do when you took this job as our cook, but—"

"I've grown very fond of the little mites. They're good helpers, the two of them. I'll keep them occupied."

"You're a wonder, Mrs. Gleason."

The trolley Addy and Susannah took to the shopping district was so crowded they had to stand the entire time, clinging to the posts for dear life. The streets in the shopping district were also jammed with people, and Addy linked arms with Susannah as they made their way to Dixon's Department Store as if swimming against a mighty current. Addy hated being bumped and buffeted by so many people and kept her bag tucked close to her side, mindful of Howard's warnings of pickpockets. She stopped in front of the window display of toys that had so fascinated Jack and Polly, wondering what to choose. Addy could've had any toy or trinket her heart desired as a girl, so she found it difficult to imagine what children who'd never owned a toy in their life might like.

"What do you suggest I buy for Jack and Polly?" she asked Susannah. "Do you remember what drew their eye the last time?"

"Well . . . I think Jack admired that fire engine. And Polly should have a doll, of course."

"Perfect." They went inside and took the elevator to the toy department on the third floor. It was decorated like a winter wonderland with twinkling lights and a locomotive that traveled on real tracks around a miniature village. Susannah seemed mesmerized by it.

"Wouldn't the children love to see this?"

"I think my husband would enjoy seeing it, too," Addy said, laughing. They selected a cast-iron fire engine for Jack with wheels that really turned, pulled by a team of cast-iron horses. For Polly, Susannah chose a small, soft, baby doll with a frilly white gown and a cherubic porcelain face. Addy smiled to herself as she paid for the purchases, imagining the fun the children would have playing with them. But in the next moment, her smile faded as she wondered what would become of the toys if the children had to return to the orphanage. No doubt, the other children would be envious. The matron may not allow them to even own toys. Somehow, no matter what it took, Addy couldn't allow that to happen. She sent up a silent prayer for their father to come home safely.

"Will you help me select a small gift for your aunt?" Addy asked when they returned to the main floor with their parcels. "Can you think of something special she might like?"

"Goodness! Everything in the store is so beautiful, I wouldn't know what to choose."

"Does she have a nice vanity set with a comb, brush, and hand mirror? These ebony ones are nice. So is this tortoiseshell set. These leather gloves are lovely, too. Which do you think she'd like?" Susannah was stroking the shining ebony with such reverence that Addy quickly decided. She chose the tortoiseshell vanity set and whispered to the clerk to discretely include a second ebony set as a surprise for Susannah.

The sun was shining as they stepped outside again, making Addy feel like skipping down the street—if it weren't so crowded! "I've never gone Christmas shopping before," she told Susannah. "I never knew it could be so much fun."

Susannah appeared shocked. "Didn't you ever have Christmas presents?"

"Oh, yes, my sisters and I would find dozens of nice things beneath the tree. But we never enjoyed the fun of shopping for other people."

"That's sad," Susannah said with a little frown. "We didn't have money to buy things, so we always made presents for each other, and for our gran and granddad. It was fun to surprise them."

"I agree, it is sad. I may have had a lot of things, but I think I missed so many special experiences. My grandmother took me to some orphanages with her, sometimes, to deliver Christmas presents, but I still grew up to be selfish and I thought it was boring." They continued down the street, heading toward a little stationery shop where Addy planned to purchase paper to wrap the gifts. She had shopped at the pretty little store before, which offered personalized engraving on elegant stationery, thank-you notes, and invitations. Her heart beat faster when she saw a sign in the window, advertising for a salesclerk. The opportunity seemed too wonderfully coincidental to pass up. "Susannah, look! They need a salesclerk! You must apply for the job."

"Me?" Her voice came out in a squeak.

"Yes. This is a wonderful little shop that has been owned by the same family for generations. It would be the perfect place to work for your first job. Let's go in and tell them you'd like to apply." Addy pulled open the door, causing a bell to tinkle, but Susannah didn't move. She stood rooted to the sidewalk as if her feet were encased in concrete. "Come on," Addy beckoned.

"I-I can't!"

She went back outside and rested her hand on the girl's shoulder. "You're ready, Susannah, I know you are. And even if they don't hire you, it will be good practice for when you apply for the next job." Addy took her hand and tried pulling her forward, but the girl didn't budge. Addy could feel her trembling.

"I can't! I'm too scared!"

"Life is filled with scary things and first times. But do you really want to be a scrub maid all your life? I know you can do this, Susannah. Trust me."

"What if I mess up?"

"Then we'll try again another day, at a different store. Come on, I'll be right beside you." She finally managed to pull Susannah into the store, imagining drag marks on the wooden floor from the girl's feet.

The owner greeted Addy by name, which should have relieved some of Susannah's fears. "What can I do for you ladies today?" she asked.

"Good morning, Mrs. Duncan. I've come for some pretty paper to wrap my Christmas presents. But I also noticed that you're looking for a salesclerk."

"Yes. It would be part-time, three days a week, at most."

"That's perfect. This is Susannah Marshall, who currently works for me. She's honest, capable, and very hard-working. She has never worked as a salesclerk before, but I've been coaching her, and I can highly recommend her for your lovely store. What must she do to apply?"

"I would be happy to hire her on your recommendation, Mrs. Forsythe. Your family has done business with us for many years, beginning with your grandmother, I believe. I was so sorry to hear of her passing."

"Thank you. We miss her dearly." Susannah seemed to

relax a bit as they spent the next few minutes exchanging information and outlining what her duties at the shop would be. She looked around at the variety of colorful paper and elegant stationery, the pens and diaries and notebooks, her eyes shining with awe. When Mrs. Duncan told her what her starting salary would be, Addy feared Susannah's knees might give way. They agreed that Susannah would begin on the Monday morning after Christmas for a trial period. Addy purchased some colorful wrapping paper, and they left the store. Susannah couldn't stop smiling.

"There. See? Aren't you glad you went in and applied?"

"I-I can't believe it! I'm going to be a real shop clerk. And, since it's only a few days a week, I can still clean for you."

"That's true," Addy said, laughing. "But no more scrubbing. You'll ruin your hands."

"I can't wait to tell my aunt the news. Are we going home, now?"

"Well, I need to stop and see my mother first. It should only take an hour or so. You're welcome to come with me, or you can go back to my town house by yourself, if you can find your way. It's up to you."

"I would like to go back." They agreed that Susannah would carry the toys and hide them from the children, and then they went their separate ways. The line of people at the trolley stop was so long, and the winter day so cold, that Addy was tempted to hire a carriage for the trip to her mother's mansion. But she remembered her vow to stay within Howard's budget, and climbed onto the crowded car for the endless ride. She found Mother in the mansion's study, working on business for the Stanhope Foundation.

"Addy! How wonderful to see you." She rose to embrace her and Addy inhaled the wonderful, familiar scent of her perfume. "What brings you here on such a cold day?"

"I've been shopping for Christmas gifts, and I thought I'd better pick up Howard's present, since you'll be leaving for Boston, soon. Are you excited about spending the holiday with Cordelia?"

"And my grandchildren, yes, of course."

"Be sure to give them my love."

Addy followed her mother to the library and to the piles of books she had set aside for Howard when Mother had moved to this smaller mansion. "I bought him a new pair of leather gloves, too, but I think he'll be surprised and pleased with these books. He always admired Grandfather's library." And being conscious of his limited budget and his wish for her not to spend her inheritance, Addy knew her frugality would make them both happy. A servant brought a tray of tea, and she and Mother sat drinking it together while the servants boxed up the books. Addy told her about Susannah's new job, and her idea for a school where young girls could learn useful skills.

"I think that's a wonderful idea. When the time comes, be sure to submit a proposal for the school to me. It sounds like something the Stanhope Foundation would be happy to support."

By the time they finished their tea, the fickle sun had vanished and it had begun to snow—large, soggy flakes that fell from a blanket of thick clouds. "I'd better go home," Addy said. "Mrs. Gleason has been caring for the children all morning."

"Before you do, there's something I want you to have. Call it an early Christmas present." She led Addy into the grand living room and pointed to the creche on the console table.

"I remember this!" The holy family, shepherds, and wise men were delicately carved and exquisitely hand-painted in fine detail. "You bought this set in Italy, didn't you?"

"Yes. Take it home with you. I'll have the servants wrap it up."

"I couldn't! It's too costly and delicate! I mean, with two small children in the house, they might break it!"

"You always admired it when you were a child, more so than Ernestine or Cordelia ever did. I think it was because your grandmother used to tell you so many Bible stories. I remember warning you never to touch it, that it might break. And I regret that, now."

"Mother, are you sure?"

"Jesus was born in a stable. His first visitors were poor shepherds. He's a savior for the everyday people."

"And for the wealthy. The three kings bowed down to Him, too."

"Take it with you, Addy. Enjoy it. And use it." Addy hugged her mother tightly.

The servants carefully wrapped and packed the creche and brought Addy's coat. Wet snowflakes continued to fall from the afternoon sky, and even if Addy could have carried all the boxes, she and the books would have been soaked before she'd even walked to the trolley stop. Mother's carriage driver took her home.

The driver carried the boxes into the town house for her, and Addy hid the books in the spare bedroom closet. She would wait until Howard was home to show the creche to him and the children. She had just finished changing her clothes when someone knocked on her bedroom door. She was surprised to see Mrs. Gleason, who rarely ventured upstairs from her kingdom in the kitchen.

"May I speak with you about something, Mrs. Forsythe?" she said in a near whisper.

"Yes, of course. Come in." The cook stepped across the threshold but would go no farther into the room, as if she'd encountered a wall of glass. The look of concern on her usually cheerful face made Addy's heart speed up. It suddenly occurred to her that she had never asked for Mrs. Gleason's permission to train Susannah to be a salesclerk—let alone to apply for a job in the busy shopping district. She braced herself, prepared to apologize for being too presumptuous.

"Susannah told me about the job, and what you've been doing for her, teaching her things, and all. I never would have imagined such a possibility, and I'm not sure I would have encouraged her to step out in such a way. She's just a farm girl, after all. And a very young one, at that."

"Mrs. Gleason, I'm so sorry if I—"

"There's no need to apologize, dear. Susannah is very excited, and I'm grateful for all your encouragement."

Addy's shoulders sagged with relief. "She's a bright girl. I'm glad she'll have a better future than scrubbing my floors."

Mrs. Gleason managed a half-smile. "Although I have to say, when I saw her prancing around with a book on her head and smiling at herself in the mirror—well, it seemed very odd to me."

"She'll make your family proud, Mrs. Gleason."

She nodded, then her smile faded, replaced by the look

of concern once again. "There's something else I need to tell you about."

"Yes?"

"For the past few days, I've noticed some food going missing. A couple of apples, some carrots, a few slices of bread. It has disappeared at odd times of the day, so I didn't think you or Mr. Forsythe had taken them."

"No, we haven't."

"I sat Jack down and told him that if he or Polly was hungry, he only needed to ask. He was welcome to almost anything. But he didn't reply. He just looked past me. And food is still disappearing." She drew a breath, then sighed. Her entire body seemed to deflate. "Now some money has gone missing, too. I keep very careful accounts of all the money you give me for groceries and such, and I always put the loose change in a little jar where it's handy for paying deliverymen, and so on. But I noticed that some dimes and nickels have disappeared from that jar. I asked Jack if he'd taken them, but again, he wouldn't answer me. He didn't deny it, but he didn't admit it, either. I'm very fond of Jack and I thought he trusted me in return. But he wouldn't talk to me about it. It was as if he was as deaf as little Polly."

Addy struggled for a reply. "I'm so sorry to hear it. I-I have no idea how to handle this, Mrs. Gleason."

"Neither do I. But I thought you should know. I talked to him about how it was wrong to steal but it didn't seem to faze him. All I could do was put the jar of change out of temptation's reach."

"Thank you for telling me. I'll talk it over with Mr. Forsythe and let you know what he thinks we should do."

Mrs. Gleason nodded sadly and hurried away. Addy knew how fond she was of Jack, and could easily imagine how hurt and disappointed she must be that he'd broken her trust. Addy felt hurt, too. She and Howard had done so much for the children. She remembered the orphanage director's warning that the orphans could be very manipulative, and felt sick inside. She hoped Howard would know what to do about the situation because she certainly didn't.

She told him about Susannah's new job as they ate their dinner in the kitchen late that evening. Once again, the children already had gone to bed. "That's wonderful, Addy! I'm happy for her. And for you. It sounds like you taught her well and gave her the confidence she needed." He smiled, raising one eyebrow, and added, "It also sounds like you're going to need a new housekeeper."

"Susannah will still work for us a few days a week. And I'm learning to do some things around the house—"

"Addy, no." His smile vanished. "I don't want you doing

the work of a maidservant. You have so many other gifts that should be used. A maid can be replaced, but you can't."

She didn't want to spoil their dinner with bad news, so she waited to tell Howard about Jack's thefts until later that night as they prepared for bed. She remembered the sadness in Mrs. Gleason's eyes as she'd stood in their bedroom doorway, and felt the pain of Jack's deception all over again. "What do you think we should we do about it, Howard?"

He sank down on the edge of the bed and stared at the quilt as if deep in thought. Then he looked up at her and said, "Nothing. I don't think there's anything we can do."

"Nothing?"

"Mrs. Gleason tried talking to him, right? And Jack is closer to her than to either of us. He knows he's done something wrong, so the next step is up to him."

"Why do you suppose he's stealing? We've given him everything he needs, haven't we?"

"Maybe." He closed his eyes for a long moment before looking up at her again. "Except for assurance about his future. He doesn't know what's going to happen to him and Polly if his father doesn't come home."

"But we're not sure about that ourselves, are we?"

"No. So, if I had to guess, I'd say that Jack might be stockpiling food and money so he can take care of Polly himself. He's a good kid, Addy, and very bright. I don't think he would steal unless he felt he had no other choice."

She went to Howard and sat beside him, wrapping her arms around him. She rested her head against his chest, listening to his strong, steady heartbeat. "I think you're right. Maybe you can have a talk with him tomorrow."

"I will, if I see an opening. But if he asks about the future, I don't have any answers for him. That's probably why he's praying so hard for his father to come home."

"I've been praying, too." She lifted her face to kiss him. "My faith is being tested to the limit, Howard. I think it's time I prayed a little harder."

CHAPTER 11

Howard had become so accustomed to rising early that he found himself wide awake before the sun came up, even though it was Saturday. He lay in bed, thinking. And worrying. Sweet Addy wanted to spend her sizable inheritance on a girls' school. And while he loved her for her generous soul, he found it hard to contemplate giving up all that money and sacrificing her future security. It seemed unwise. He'd promised to think about her idea, and he had. In fact, he'd thought of little else. He still didn't have an answer for her.

Howard was reminded every day of how much Addy had given up in order to marry him—a palatial mansion, a staff of servants, a life of ball gowns and parties and wealth. She had never been forced to travel by public trolley in her life until she'd married him. The money she'd inherited from her father was her safety net against an uncertain future, and Howard balked at the idea of spending it. As the room grew lighter with the rising sun, he spotted the photograph of Addy's grandmother, Junietta Stanhope, on the bedroom dresser. Howard sympathized with Neal Galloway, an impoverished immigrant who had fallen in love with wealthy Junietta. Like himself, Neal had wanted to give the woman he loved a life of luxury, and he had decided his only recourse was to seek his fortune in the California gold fields. Instead, Neal had died in a shipwreck en route to California. Junietta insisted she would have rather had the man she loved than a life of wealth without him. Addy said the same thing about Howard.

She was right; Howard knew she was. The Bible said to give and it would be given to him, full measure, pressed down, running over. He had known Addy's grandmother— a truly remarkable and generous woman—and he applauded Addy's decision to be like her. He had spent some time at work yesterday, figuring out how he could make Addy's greathearted idea work and still preserve her inheritance for the future, but couldn't see how.

Addy stirred and rolled over to face him, opening her eyes, and smiling her beautiful smile. "Good morning, Mr. Forsythe. I'm so glad it's Saturday and I can wake up beside you."

He moved closer to her. "I'm glad, too, Mrs. Forsythe." She had plaited her long hair in a braid for the night, and he tickled her face with the end of it until she laughed.

"I have a surprise for you when you're ready for breakfast," she said. "Two surprises. Are you hungry?"

"Hungry for your kisses." He stole a few.

Howard couldn't imagine what Addy's surprise might be, but when she scooped portions of perfectly scrambled eggs onto all their plates a while later, he was impressed. "You're a woman of many talents," he said, taking a bite. "Delicious!"

"Thank you. And maybe I'll have another surprise for you next Saturday."

"Pancakes!" Jack said, then covered his mouth. His blue eyes were wide as he looked up at Addy in fear for giving away her secret.

"That's all right. I know it's hard to keep secrets." She sat down at the table with them and spread jam on a piece of toast she'd made. Jack and Polly gobbled their breakfast as if they hadn't eaten in a week—or perhaps they were afraid they'd have nothing to eat tomorrow. The idea saddened Howard.

"And now for my second surprise," Addy said. She rose from the table and untied her apron. "Everyone come upstairs to the parlor. My mother gave us an early Christmas present." Howard swallowed his last sip of tea and followed her and the curious children. Addy produced a box from where she'd hidden it in the dining room and set it in the middle of the parlor floor. Jack and Polly sank down beside it, and Howard knelt with them. "It's not a toy, mind you, but something that will remind us of what Christmas truly means. Go ahead, open it. Carefully."

Howard undid the cardboard flaps, and he and the children pulled out and unwrapped the pieces one by one, revealing magnificently painted figures of the holy family, shepherds, and wise men. "These look very expensive, Addy. Are you sure we should be handling them?"

"I'm positive. The children will remember to be careful, won't you? I thought we could display it on the parlor table. There's even a wooden stable to place the figures in." She sat back, smiling as she watched. Howard couldn't get over how carefully and reverently the children handled the figures. He wondered if little Polly understood what they represented. When she found the baby Jesus, she cupped Him in her little hands and held Him to her cheek.

"That's what I always wanted to do with the Christ child," Addy said softly.

When the creche was fully unpacked and the figures placed on the table exactly where the children had decided they should go, Addy sent Jack and Polly off to get dressed. "Don't you think we should put that up higher?" Howard asked. "On the mantel, maybe?" Addy shook her head.

"I want the children to be able to see it." She seemed very sure. "So, what do we have planned for today?" she asked.

"I've only just decided, but with Christmas four days away, I think I should go back to Jack's tenement and talk to his neighbors and the building superintendent again. I want to do everything I can to make sure Mr. Thomas knows where to find his children. Maybe I'll go to the shipyard again, too."

"I can be ready to go shortly." He put his hand on her arm, stopping her, then lowered his voice.

"I'd rather you stayed here with the children. Or at least with Polly. I'm worried it might be too hard on her to go back to where her mother died. She must have been terrified to be left all alone after the authorities took Jack away. And then to be taken to that terrible asylum." He shuddered, remembering. "I'll take Jack, if he wants to come, just to reassure him that we're doing everything we can."

Addy looked panicked. "What in the world will I do with Polly while you're gone? I don't know how to take care of a child!"

"What does Mrs. Gleason do with her?"

"I don't know. I guess she lets Polly help her. Washing dishes and such. Susannah takes her outside to play."

Howard kissed her. "I won't be long."

Polly cried and fussed when she saw Jack getting ready to leave without her. It was an eerie, plaintive wail of mourning, like a wounded animal's. Somehow, Jack managed to calm her without words. Addy was standing in the doorway, holding Polly on her hip as Howard waved goodbye to them, and he and Jack started walking toward the trolley stop. The sight of Addy holding a child, much less scrambling eggs earlier this morning, haunted him. He knew she would gladly do all these domestic chores, thinking it would please him. But she dreamed of starting a girls' school, and he wanted her to follow her dreams.

He shook his head to clear his thoughts, listening as Jack peppered him with questions. He was interested in every aspect of the streetcar ride, where the trolley stops were, and where to change to the next line, and to how to read the schedule. "Can I put the money for our fare in the slot?" he asked as they boarded.

"Sure." Howard handed him the coins. He was a bright little boy, that was for certain. But the dilemma of what would become of the children if their father didn't return home continued to haunt Howard. To be honest, he doubted that Jack's father would come home. Should he and Addy adopt them? It would have to be Addy's decision because she would have the biggest share of the work in raising them. As the trolley continued its stop-and-go journey through traffic-filled streets, Howard scrambled to think of a different solution. He tapped Jack's shoulder. The boy was perched on the edge of the seat, peering intently out the window, but he turned to Howard.

"What?"

"I need you to do me a favor and think very hard, Jack. Do you remember any other relatives in your family? Aunts or uncles or grandparents? Did your parents ever talk about their families? Or did anyone ever come over to visit?" Jack squinted his eyes as if concentrating hard.

"I can't remember." He looked tearful.

Howard ruffled his hair. "That's all right, Jack. Don't worry about it."

They knocked on every apartment door in Jack's former tenement, explaining the children's situation again, and passing out Howard's calling cards. The look of longing and hope on Jack's face when he peered inside the apartment where he'd once lived nearly broke Howard's heart. The same elderly Russian woman had answered the door, shaking her head and refusing his card. Howard guessed that she didn't understand a word he said.

"Tell her she's gotta give us our house back when Papa comes home," Jack said after the door closed in their faces.

"I can't do that. We'll find a different apartment for you. A better one." Howard could have kicked himself for offering hope where there probably wasn't any. They descended the dank basement steps to speak with the superintendent again. "Good morning, Mr. Pawloski. Do you remember us?"

"Yeah. He's the kid who's waiting for his father."

"Right. We found Jack's sister in an orphanage, but we're still trying to locate any other family members. Are you sure there was nothing left from their apartment that might give us a clue?"

Once again, the man turned angry and defensive. "I watched the police go through the kid's stuff, looking for things like that, and I'm telling you, the people around here grab whatever's left over when someone moves on."

No doubt Pawloski had taken his share of things, too. Howard decided not to rile the man by pressing the matter. "You may recall that Mr. Thomas took a job onboard a ship. Jack remembers seeing him off at the dock nearby. He's expected home for Christmas. Here's my card. If he comes back to this apartment looking for his children, please send him to this address." Once again, he slipped the man some money along with the card.

Jack stood in the tenement's tiny vestibule after they'd climbed back up the stairs as if reluctant to leave. Howard found it hard to imagine that the boy considered this dingy, drafty place his home, or that he'd want his depressing apartment back. Howard and Addy's modest town house must seem like a mansion in comparison. A huge step up. Yet Addy had taken a huge step down to live there with him, compared to her mansion. Howard cringed every time he thought about it. He watched Jack's face as he caressed the splintery handrail and realized that this tenement, shabby as it was, probably held all the memories Jack had of his parents and their life as a family.

A verse of Scripture that his mother often referred to when money was tight floated through Howard's memory. Something about a meal of vegetables in a loving home being better than the finest cuts of meat with hatred. Addy had told him the terrible stories of her great-grandfather's greed, and the people he'd intentionally ruined. She'd shared her memories of how vast and cold the mansion had seemed, separating her family members from each other. He'd seen it for himself when he'd visited there. She hadn't lacked for material things, but for love and a sense of family. And he could give those things to her in abundance, no matter where they lived. He reached for Jack's hand.

"Come on, son. Let's go back to the dock and ask about the ships that are due to arrive."

"Can we go to the church, too? And light a candle?"

"Sure." Jack held his hand tightly as they walked toward the church. The snow, which seemed so white and pristine in Howard's neighborhood, lay in gray dirty mounds, coated with a layer of soot and blowing garbage. "The candle isn't magic, you know," Howard said before opening the church door. "It's not as if you can light one and make a wish, and God will give you whatever you want."

Jack looked up at him in surprise. "That's what Mama did."

"No, I think she probably said a prayer for your father, and the candle was a symbol of that prayer. God knows all our needs before we even ask. And He knows the best way to answer our prayers, even if it isn't always what we wish for."

Jack seemed unconvinced. He released Howard's hand and ran up the aisle to the flickering rack of candles. Howard watched him light one, then kneel to pray, his forehead pressed against his folded hands. Howard sighed and went to talk with the priest. The man shook his head at the seeming futility of their search and promised to give Howard's card to Mr. Thomas if he came.

Afterward, Howard walked through the gray snow to the shipyard with Jack, his toes turning numb with cold. He wiggled them inside his shoes as he waited to speak with the owner again. The man remembered them and knew why they had come. "All the ships we were expecting before Christmas have docked except for one. It's due to arrive tomorrow."

"And no sign of Mr. Thomas?"

"We put your card in the pay packets of all the sailors named Thomas but none of them seemed to know what you were talking about. Sorry."

"Thanks for trying."

"Like I said, your missing man may have signed on with a foreign ship."

"I appreciate your help. Have a Merry Christmas."

Howard had to face the possibility that the children's father might have deliberately abandoned his family. Perhaps the rosy picture Jack painted of a loving father had sprung from a hopeful imagination of how he wished his homelife had been. Discouragement made Howard's steps heavy as they climbed aboard the streetcar for the long, tedious ride home. He could well imagine how Jack must feel. With his future uncertain, no wonder the boy was stealing food from the pantry and change from the money jar.

"I have one more errand to run, Jack. Do you want me to take you to the town house first? Are you getting tired? Cold?"

"Where're you going?"

Howard managed a smile. "I want to stop at a tree lot and buy a Christmas tree. To surprise the ladies."

"Okay," Jack said with a shrug. "I'll go."

"Did you ever have a Christmas tree before?"

"No, but I seen them in places."

They finally got off and walked two blocks toward the lot. Howard had passed it every day on his way to and from work and hoped they still had some good trees left this close to Christmas. As he prepared to cross the street, he noticed, for the first time, a vacant house across from the Christmas tree lot. It had a *For Sale* sign in the window. The large home looked as though it had once belonged to a wealthy family before the bustling neighborhood had sprung up around it and the upper class had built new houses farther north. The Gothic stone structure seemed out of place on a street lined with small shops—a grocer, a fruit seller, a cobbler, a tailor shop. The modest stores had apartments on the floors above them.

"Hold on a minute, Jack. I want to check out this house." He bounded up the steps to the front porch and peered through the windows at the large, empty rooms. The house stood on a corner, so Howard circled around to the rear, looking inside every window he could reach. He ended up in front again, and decided to go into the crammed little grocery store next door. The owner was dusting the tall shelves of goods behind the counter. "Good morning. Do you know anything about that house for sale next door?"

"Not much. It's been vacant for a year or two. Used to be a 'finishing school' until the two old spinsters who ran it passed on. I always wondered what it was that needed finishing," he said with a laugh.

Howard's heart pounded with excitement. It would be perfect for Addy's school. He wondered how much it cost. How much of her inheritance would be eaten up if she bought it and restored it? Would there be any money left for Addy's future? He paused for a long moment, deliberating, while Jack wandered a few feet away, eyeing a display of apples. Howard watched the boy, and for a moment, it looked as though he might be thinking of pocketing one. Without a home, Jack and Polly would have little choice except to steal in order to live. Then the boy saw Howard watching him, and shoved his hands in his pockets.

"Are we still getting a tree?" he asked.

"Yes. In a minute."

Suddenly, Howard saw himself in Jack. The boy feared an unknown future and had been stealing to try to secure a future for himself and Polly. Was Howard also 'stealing' because of his fear of the future? By hoarding Addy's inheritance, he would be stealing a better future from all the young women she wanted to help. Didn't he trust God?

Howard nearly laughed out loud as all his anxious fretting about money and the future came into focus. God was a trustworthy Father. He loved Addy as much as Howard did. He could be trusted to provide for her future. Peace flooded Howard's heart.

"Can I get you something?" the grocer asked.

"Hmm? Pardon? Yes. Yes! You wouldn't happen to sell popcorn, would you?"

"Decorating a Christmas tree, are you?"

"That's right."

The man scooped dried corn from a bin and showed it to Howard before pouring it into a bag. "This enough?"

"Give us two scoops. If I remember correctly, my brothers and I always ate more popcorn than we ever strung." He paid the man and took Jack's hand again.

"Merry Christmas," the man called as they opened the door.

Howard turned back. "Yes. Merry Christmas!"

Christmas. When God showed His great love by giving the world His most precious gift—His Son. Howard went outside into the cold again, happier than he'd felt in months. No doubt he would still worry about the future and agonize over not being a good provider for his beloved Addy. But God knew the future, and that was enough.

"Let's find a Christmas tree, Jack."

They searched through the lot. Some were too tall, some too short. Too full or too spindly. At last, they found the perfect one and negotiated a good price. He tipped the young lad who pushed it to the town house for him in a wheelbarrow and helped him and Jack wrestle it through the front door.

"Oh, my! It's so big. Is it going to fit?" Addy asked.

"We'll find out in a minute." They moved a chair and an end table to make room for it in the parlor window, facing the street. Polly seemed frightened by it at first, but Jack gently nudged her closer for a better look. He put a branch to his nose, sniffing dramatically, then motioned for her to do the same. She copied him, inhaling the scent, then beamed a wide smile. Polly reached to touch the tree, then drew back when the needles prickled her hand. She and Jack laughed, then she reached to smell it again.

Howard stood in the doorway with his arm around Addy, watching them. He marveled at the boy's tender patience. "There are so few trees in the children's neighborhood, it's little wonder this is a novelty."

"Any luck at the tenement or the shipyard?" she whispered.

Howard shook his head. "What do you say we get busy and start decorating this tree?"

Addy looked up at him. "Where do we start? I've never decorated one before."

"You're joking."

"Our trees were always enormous, and they had to be decorated perfectly. Mother hired a crew of florists and experts to do it."

"Astonishing. Well, we'll start with this." He held up the paper bag, shaking it so the corn rattled.

"What is that?"

"Corn. We can pop it and string it together to make decorations for the tree."

"Do you know how to pop corn?" she asked, as if such a thing was a complicated mystery.

Howard laughed and lifted her up, twirling her around before kissing her and setting her down again. "Come on. I'll teach you."

PART 4

THE CANDLE OF PEACE

Peace on earth, and mercy mild,
God and sinners reconciled!
CHARLES WESLEY, "Hark! The Herald Angels Sing"

Peace I leave with you; my peace I give you.
I do not give to you as the world gives.
Do not be troubled and do not be afraid.

JOHN 14:27

CHAPTER 12

Howard arrived at church with Addy and the children a little early on Sunday morning, so he decided to wait in the parsonage, next door. His mom welcomed them inside, opening her arms to the children. "My, don't you darlings look fresh and lovely this morning! May I give you a hug?" They went to her without hesitation, just as they did to Mrs. Gleason. "Look at these beautiful hair ribbons!" She held up the ends of Polly's braids, smiling as she met the little girl's gaze. Polly beamed in return.

"She understands so much," Addy said. "I spent yesterday morning with her, and she's a bright little girl."

"Aye, I expect she is. Just like her brother. By the way, Howard, your dad wants Jack and Polly to light the Advent candles in church this morning." She stood again and fastened her hat to her hair with a long pin.

"Are you sure, Mom? They lit the candles last Sunday, too."

"I know. But everyone in the congregation knows their story, now. We're all praying for Mr. Thomas's safe return."

Howard wished he could believe that their father really would return, but he was afraid to hope. "Which candle is it this week?" he asked.

"Peace," his mom replied. "It's the candle of peace."

Later, in church, Howard lifted Polly in his arms as he and Addy helped the children light the Advent candles. Polly felt more relaxed in his embrace, and he thought the girl was starting to trust him.

"Peace on earth and mercy mild," the congregation sang. "God and sinners, reconciled." In his sermon, his dad explained that the peace Jesus came to bring wasn't peace from conflict and war, but peace with God.

"We find peace in the assurance that in all life's changes, we can trust in an unchanging God," he told them. "There is peace in letting go of our plans and embracing God's plans. Jesus, the Prince of Peace said, 'Peace I leave with you; my peace I give you. I do not give to you as the world gives. Do not let your hearts be troubled and do not be afraid.'"

His words reminded Howard once again that he could find peace in trusting God with his and Addy's futures. He reached for Addy's hand. She looked up at him as she squeezed his in return.

After the service, his mom hugged the children again before saying goodbye. "You did such a wonderful job with the candles, both of you. There's only one more candle to light and that's the Christ Candle in the center of the wreath. We'll light that one on Christmas Day. Then you're all invited to the parsonage for Christmas dinner."

"Can my papa come, too?" Jack asked. "He's coming home for Christmas, you know."

"Of course, he's welcome. I would love to meet him."

When they returned to the town house, Addy served lunch from the food Mrs. Gleason had left, then Jack and Polly asked to go outside to play. Howard stood at the window with Addy, watching them frolic in the snow. "I forgot to ask how you managed to keep little Polly occupied while Jack and I were gone yesterday," he said.

"I was very nervous, at first. Being with small children seems to come naturally to some people, like your mother and Mrs. Gleason, but it's very new to me."

"They've had years of practice."

"Yes. Well, Polly and I washed the breakfast dishes together, and she liked standing beside me on a chair and playing in the soapy water. It made me wonder if she remembered doing that with her mother."

"Hm. They're so young. I wonder what memories they do have of their parents. Jack seemed reluctant to leave the tenement yesterday. It's hard to believe, but I think that place must feel like home to him."

"I don't think they feel completely at home here, yet. After we finished the dishes, I took Polly upstairs with me. I wish we could convince her and Jack to sleep up there instead of the little maid's room."

"That small, plain space must feel more familiar to them."

"I suppose. I can't imagine what they would think of Mother's mansion."

Howard laughed. "The same thing I thought when I first went there—it's a fairytale castle!"

"Anyway, I learned that Polly likes pretty, colorful things. She was fascinated by the gowns in my wardrobe. She wanted to feel all the textures, the satins and silks and nubby wools. She smiled when I tickled her with a bit of fur. I showed her my jewelry and we tried on some of the necklaces and bracelets. She almost managed a smile when she sat at my dressing table and looked at herself in the mirror. She let me brush and braid her hair."

"She is a pretty little thing. So wispy and delicate. She reminds me of one of the fairies in my childhood storybooks."

"I decided to take a walk with her to that little notions shop a few blocks away and buy her some hair ribbons. We bundled up—and I've noticed that the children don't seem to mind the cold as much as I do."

"You're right. Look at them out there. And it's a cold day!" Jack and Polly were chasing each other around the tiny yard and darting among the bushes. "There's no place like this to play in their old neighborhood."

"Polly was fascinated by all the different colored ribbons in the shop, so I let her pick out some. We bought some Christmas ribbons too, to tie up the packages. We had a nice morning together. The time passed more quickly than I thought it would."

"I was thinking as we lit those Advent candles this morning that we've experienced everything they symbolize this season, haven't we? Hope, Love, Joy—"

"But maybe not Peace. I wish I felt more at peace about the children's future."

"I know. Me, too. But it isn't Christmas yet, Addy. Let's wait and see what happens."

MONDAY, DECEMBER 23

Addy sat at the kitchen table, pressing raisins into the soft cookie dough to make eyes and buttons on a pan of gingerbread cookies. She had helped Mrs. Gleason cream butter and sugar together, and had enjoyed sharing the warmth and laughter with the others in the kitchen. It was an experience she'd never had in her childhood. The heavenly aroma of gingerbread filled the house.

"Don't forget to poke little holes in the tops," Mrs. Gleason reminded her. "We'll string a ribbon through them and tie them on the Christmas tree."

"Can I eat this cookie?" Jack asked, holding it up. "His arm is broken."

Mrs. Gleason planted her hands on her hips, pretending to be stern, but love shone in her eyes. "Well, I suppose. But share it with your sister, and then that's the last one. At the rate you're eating them, Jackie-boy, there won't be any left to hang on the Christmas tree."

"And remember, we want to bring some to the parsonage on Christmas Day," Addy said. She finished decorating the last one and handed the cookie sheet to Mrs. Gleason, who had just removed a batch from the oven. "You don't need to worry about cooking a Christmas dinner for us, Mrs. Gleason. We're invited to celebrate the day with Howard's family. And it's a tradition for servants to take Boxing Day off, so I hope you have a wonderful holiday with your family."

"Thank you, dear. I'll be sure to leave enough food to last until I return."

"What about you, Susannah?" Addy asked. "Are you going home to the farm for Christmas?" Susannah had been floating around the town house with her head in the clouds for the past few days as if dreaming of her new job in the stationery store.

"Yes, ma'am. I told Mama my good news and she ordered a new skirt and shirtwaist for me from the Sears catalogue for my first day of work."

"I'm sure you'll look lovely, Susannah. I can't wait to hear all about your new job."

They cleared off the kitchen table when the cookies were finished, and Susannah taught Addy and the children how to make Christmas ornaments using leftover wrapping paper. She helped them fold it into little fans to form bodies and wings, creating clever little angels. They used some of the acorns they had found for the angels' heads. Susannah also taught them to fold and cut snowflakes from plain white paper. Last of all, she tied ribbons onto some of the pine cones they'd collected and "frosted" them with Epsom salts to make them look pretty.

"You're so talented with things like this," Addy told her.

Susannah shrugged. "It's nothing special. We used to make ornaments like these at home for our tree. All of us kids would tramp through the woods with Papa to cut one down, then we'd decorate it together with the things we'd made."

"That sounds like fun. The popcorn strings we made on Saturday didn't turn out very well, but the children had a good time trying. Howard did, too."

Susannah had helped Addy wrap the toys for the children and the boxes of books for Howard, tying them with pretty ribbon. They had carried them downstairs and hidden them in the broom closet until Christmas Eve when Addy would put them beneath the tree. She gave Susannah and Mrs. Gleason their wrapped presents before they went home for the day. "Remember, no peeking until Christmas."

"That goes for you, too," Mrs. Gleason said. Addy had spotted Susannah tucking some wrapped packages beneath the tree. "Have a very Merry Christmas, Mrs. Forsythe. And I'll be asking the Good Lord to please bring that lost father home to be with his children."

Howard had promised to come home from work early this evening, so Addy and the children waited for him to arrive to decorate the tree with their new ornaments. He inhaled dramatically after walking through the door and said, "Mmm! It smells like Christmas in here!"

The children danced around him, holding up some of the ornaments they'd made. "Look what we made for the tree!" Jack said. "It's going to look beautiful!"

Howard bent to look at the things the children were showing him. "You made these, Jack? Wow! I'm impressed."

"We made gingerbread men, too. Some are to hang on the tree but some are to eat!"

"Ah! That's why it smells so good in here. Give me a minute to change my clothes and we'll start decorating that tree." He paused on his way to the stairs to give Addy a kiss. "You've been busy today."

"We have Susannah and Mrs. Gleason to thank for all this. But I did help, a little."

She joined him and the children as they hung the ornaments, with Howard lifting Jack and Polly to reach the higher branches. Addy had no memories of doing fun things like this with her father, or even sitting on his lap. He was always a distant figure, someone she was in awe of. She had wanted to earn his approval and attention, yet hadn't known how. She realized, as she watched Howard and the children, that she'd always pictured God to be the same as her father— remote and uninvolved. She was only beginning to see Him as a kind and loving father Who desired to be close to His children. Like the figures in the manger scene Mother had given her, Jesus didn't need to be kept at a distance, but enjoyed and loved.

Howard stepped back for a moment to stand beside her. "Well, what do you think?"

The tree was a little lopsided and had a bare patch on one side. The handmade angels and snowflakes were scattered unevenly on the branches. The puny strings of popcorn looked half-eaten. Addy laughed at the sight, then spoke the truth. "It's the loveliest Christmas tree I've ever had."

TUESDAY, DECEMBER 24

On Christmas Eve, Jack and Polly spent so much time standing by the front window, watching and waiting for their father, that Howard finally moved his comfortable reading chair there so they could sit down. Addy noticed that Polly had taken the carved figure of Jesus from the creche and was holding it tightly in her hand all day. When it was time to leave for the Christmas Eve candlelight service, Addy didn't have the heart to make her give it up.

Jack balked when it was time to put on his coat, refusing to go to the service at all. "What if Papa comes while we're gone? I need to stay here."

"We won't be away for very long," Howard assured him. "I'll write a note for him and leave it on the front door. Do you know if your father can read?"

"He can, but—"

"You have a Heavenly Father too, Jack. Christmas is a special time when we worship Him and thank Him for the gift He gave us. Now, put your coat on. We're all going to church."

Addy kept a close eye on Jack until they were finally in the carriage, fearing he might hide somewhere in the house where they couldn't find him. She usually loved everything about the traditional Christmas Eve candlelight service—the familiar carols and scriptures, the softly flickering candlelight that bathed the sanctuary as everyone in the congregation held a lit candle. But Jack's unease distracted her.

"Advent is the time for watching and waiting for the Christ child," Pastor Forsythe said in his sermon. "The world watched and waited for the Savior, who was promised to Adam and Eve in the Garden of Eden. Their sin plunged the world into darkness. But the angel's message to the shepherds on that first Christmas was good news for all people. A Savior had been born! Christ the Lord! The light of the world!" He paused as the lights in the sanctuary dimmed.

"Our world is still in darkness without Christ. But Jesus told His followers that we also bring light into the world." As he spoke, the flame was passed from person to person until the sanctuary was no longer in darkness. "Let your light shine before men, that they may see your good deeds and praise your Father in heaven."

It was what Addy wanted to do more than anything else—to shine a light, to make a difference. She held up her candle and sang the words of the familiar carol as the service ended:

Silent night! Holy night!
Son of God, love's pure light
Radiant beams from Thy holy face
With the dawn of redeeming grace,
Jesus, Lord, at Thy birth!
Jesus, Lord, at Thy birth!

Jack tugged on Howard's hand as they mingled with people after the service, gazing up at him with his wide blue eyes as if silently pleading with him to hurry. Addy knew he was eager to return home. "We should go," she whispered to Howard. He nodded, understanding.

All the way home, Addy hoped and prayed that they

would find Mr. Thomas waiting for them at the town house. But there was no Christmas Eve miracle. Jack's disappointment showed in the defeated way he slumped onto the chair, his eyes shining with tears. Addy didn't know what to say to comfort him. Polly had fallen asleep in Howard's arms on the way home, so he carried her downstairs and put her to bed. While he was gone, Addy took the presents she'd hidden out of the broom closet and put them beneath the tree. "Can you help me, Jack? Quickly, before Mr. Forsythe comes back?"

"Who are these for?" Jack asked as he helped her lift the boxes of books.

"These three are for Mr. Forsythe. But this one is for you, and this one is for Polly. We'll open them tomorrow morning on Christmas Day."

"What about a present for Papa?"

Did it show her lack of faith that Addy hadn't thought to buy a present for him? Jack was so filled with hope, so certain his father would be here tomorrow, opening presents with them. And while Addy didn't want to crush Jack's hopes, she was concerned that his disappointment would devastate him. How could she strike a balance?

Before she could reply, Jack said, "Papa can have my present if there isn't one for him."

His generosity touched her. She blinked away tears. "You won't have to do that. This present is for your papa." She showed him the wrapped box with the gloves she had purchased for Howard, knowing he wouldn't mind.

"What's inside?"

"It's a surprise, like all Christmas presents should be."

Howard came upstairs just then and beckoned to Jack. "Come on, son. You need to go to bed, too. I'll leave a light burning up here in the front hallway for your papa."

"Will you say prayers with me?"

"I'd be happy to." Howard was gone a long time before finally rejoining Addy in the parlor, sinking down on the sofa beside her. "He's finally asleep."

Addy snuggled close, listening as the fire hissed and crackled in the parlor stove. "I'm worried about tomorrow, Howard. I don't know if I'll be able to sleep."

"I'm worried, too."

"I've grown to love Jack and Polly, but I wish we had more time alone, with just the two of us, before taking on the responsibility of a family."

He sighed. "I know. In church tonight, I found myself hoping that someone from the congregation would step forward and offer to adopt them. Everyone has heard their story."

"Tell me the truth. Do you really think their father will come tomorrow?"

He hesitated, then sighed again. "Honestly? No, I don't. But I do know that God has a plan for Jack and Polly."

"Well, I hope He shows us what it is—and soon."

CHAPTER 13

Howard awoke to the sound of church bells ringing in the distance, all over the city, announcing Christmas Day. He sat up and looked at the time, surprised to see that it was nearly eight o'clock.

"What's wrong?" Addy asked when he tossed back the covers and climbed out of bed.

"I overslept. We'll have to hurry if we want to have time to eat breakfast, open presents, get dressed, and get to my parents' house for the Christmas Day church service, then dinner. I'm surprised the children aren't up, clamoring to open their presents. My brothers and I could hardly wait for sunrise to wake Mom and Dad."

"Polly and Jack probably never had any Christmas presents to open, before."

"Maybe not," he said as he put on his robe. "I'm guessing that if they're awake, they're already looking out the front window and watching for their father, not looking at their presents."

Addy rose as well and put on her dressing gown. Howard loved the way she looked in the morning with her hair in a long braid, messy from the night's sleep. He forgot about everything else and took her in his arms, holding her close, kissing her. "I love waking up to you every morning, beautiful lady."

"Merry Christmas, darling. Our first one together."

"Yes. Merry Christmas." He wanted to linger and hold her longer, but the clamoring church bells prodded him forward. "Well, if the children aren't awake by now, those bells will do the trick. I'll go down and stoke the fires."

He descended the stairs and peered into the parlor. The chair Howard had placed beside the window was vacant, the packages beneath the tree unopened. He went down to the kitchen and took a moment to stoke the kitchen stove so they could make tea, then peeked into the children's bedroom.

They were gone!

Howard's heart thumped against his ribs. The bed had been neatly made. The hooks where they hung their coats were empty. He checked the back door and found it unlocked. He yanked open the door and looked all around the backyard, but there was no sign of the children. He raced up to the front hallway again, startling Addy who was just coming down the stairs. "What's wrong?"

He pulled open the front door, hoping to see them huddled on the steps, watching and waiting, but they weren't there. He closed the door again and leaned against it. "They're gone, Addy. Polly and Jack are gone!"

"Gone? Where? They don't have any place to go!"

"I know." Howard ran his fingers through his hair, wishing he had done more to reassure them that they would be taken care of if their father didn't return. He should have let them know that they wouldn't be separated or sent back to the orphanage. Now it was too late.

"It's freezing outside, Howard. And they're so little! Should we notify the police?"

"I doubt they'll be concerned about two penniless orphans since there are hundreds more of them in orphanages and living in the streets. Especially if they learn that Jack has run away before."

"Let's get dressed. We have to search for them, Howard. I don't care how cold it is or how long it takes."

"I agree. They're walking, so they couldn't have gone far. Surely someone will have noticed two small children all by themselves. Come on." He headed for the stairs, wanting to take them two at a time, then halted midway. "Addy, the tenement! I'll bet they're heading back to the tenement!"

"How would they get all the way there? It's much too far to walk."

"I should have known," he said, slapping his forehead. "Jack was paying very close attention when we went there last Saturday. He asked all kinds of questions about riding the trolley. I should have guessed!"

"The missing money was probably for trolley fare!"

"Yes, and the missing food. He must have been planning this for some time."

"Let's hurry," she said, prodding him the rest of the way upstairs. She was already loosening her braid to brush out her hair. "I can't bear thinking of them all on their own in this huge city. And in such cold temperatures."

"I'll head straight to the tenement to look for them. You wait here in case—"

"I'm not waiting here. We'll search for them together."

"Listen, Addy . . ." He wanted to wrap her in blankets,

and make her stay home where she'd be safe and warm. It was hard for him not to insist. But Addy was her own person, a woman he loved and respected. She had a right to make up her own mind. "All right. I'll run out and hire a carriage, then come back for you."

The drive to the tenement seemed endless, even though there was very little traffic on Christmas morning. It was cold enough inside the carriage to see their breath, and Howard was glad Addy had thought to bring a blanket. When he had told the driver where he wanted to go, the man had looked surprised. "Are you sure you want to go there? On Christmas Day?"

"Yes, and if you could wait a moment while we run inside, you can bring us back here again, afterward."

What would he do if the children weren't there?

Howard would think about that later.

Only a handful of kids were playing in the street in front of the tenement. None of them was Polly or Jack. Smoke curled from every chimney on the dingy block of tenements, settling low in the frigid air. Soot turned the white snow gray. Howard hurried inside the building with Addy right behind him. "Jack?" he shouted. "Jack, are you here?" An apartment door on the ground floor opened and a man peered out. Howard sprinted up the stairs, mindful of the broken step, holding his breath.

And there they were.

Polly and Jack sat huddled on the floor in the drafty hallway outside their old apartment. Howard couldn't speak, relieved and angry at the same time. Addy brushed past him and knelt to encircle Polly with her arms.

"We were so worried about you!" She cupped Polly's hands in her own to warm them. Her little fingers were curled around the figure of baby Jesus. "You're so cold!" Addy said.

Howard fought to control his temper, which had been stoked hotter from worry. "Jack! What were you thinking? You brought your sister all this way by yourself? What if you'd gotten lost? Anything could have happened—including freezing to death!"

Jack crossed his arms and lifted his chin. "We're waiting for Papa."

A few more doors opened. Howard held up his hands to reassure the curious neighbors that all was well before turning back to Jack. "Look, everyone promised to tell your papa where you were. They have copies of my address. So does the building superintendent." The boy didn't reply. Howard noticed his bulging pockets and guessed they were stuffed with the missing food. Jack had planned thoroughly.

"Please, come home with us, Jack," Addy said. "It's Christmas. You haven't opened your presents."

He shook his head. "Papa is coming home today. He promised! Polly and I need to wait here for him."

Howard offered Jack his hand. "Come on. It's cold in this hallway. We have a carriage waiting. Your father will find us at the town house."

Jack's arms stayed tightly folded across his chest. "Polly and me ain't leaving."

Addy stood and tried to lift Polly in her arms, but she hunched down and snuggled closer to her brother, clinging to him. "Now what?" Addy asked.

"I don't know. We can't force them to come with us but we can't leave them here all alone, either. I suppose we could wait with them, but my parents are expecting us for Christmas dinner."

"I agree we should wait with them. Can we get a message to your parents, somehow?"

"We would have to go there and tell them what happened. Let them know we aren't coming."

"I'll stay here while you go."

"I don't want to leave you here all alone, Addy." And yet he didn't want her to travel to the parsonage by herself, either.

"I'll be fine."

It would be no use arguing with her. Of the two choices,

she would be safer—and slightly warmer—staying here. "I'll be back as quickly as I can." He brought her the blanket from the carriage before leaving.

The traffic was heavier now, with people coming and going to church on Christmas Day. Howard made it to the parsonage just as the morning service was letting out. His mother looked relieved to see him. "What happened?" she asked, raising her voice to be heard above the clanging church bells. "We were worried when we didn't see you in church."

Howard quickly explained the situation. "I came to tell you we won't be here for dinner. I need to get back. I left Addy and the children all alone. I have a carriage waiting."

"Well, ask the driver to wait ten more minutes. You aren't leaving here empty-handed. I made enough food for an army."

Howard smiled. "You always do."

"Take the ham and the rolls and the pies. And the parishioners have given us all sorts of gifts, too—cakes and cookies and fruit baskets. You can share them with the other families in the tenement." She was grabbing boxes and baskets and tins as she spoke, pointing for Howard to help her pack what looked like a great quantity of food. He began feeling anxious as he thought about leaving Addy all alone, but he could see that his mother was right. If he and Addy were going to wait at the tenement with the children all day, they may as well share the bounty of food with whoever was hungry. He made several trips, carrying everything to the waiting carriage.

"I wonder if they could use some clothing, too?" she asked after Howard had carried the final load. "The charity bin is full. Take it. There are some winter coats in there, too, I think."

He would pass near his town house on the way back, so Howard asked the driver to stop there. He quickly packed up all the food, cookies, and pies Mrs. Gleason had prepared for them for the next few days. He grabbed plates and utensils so Addy and the children could have a picnic, then headed to the tenement. The aroma of glazed ham and apple pie filled the carriage as the horses clopped through the streets.

"How much do I owe you for going to all this extra trouble for me?" he asked the driver when they arrived. "And on Christmas Day, no less."

"Just give me what we agreed on."

"But—"

"I see what you're doing, helping these poor people, and I think it's a fine idea. Merry Christmas." He even helped Howard carry everything inside.

Addy decided she may as well sit down while she waited for Howard to return. The splintery floor was filthy, and she saw spiderwebs and dead insects in the corners, but she steeled herself and sat down anyway, leaning her back against the wall like Jack was doing. She pulled Polly onto her lap. Addy wished she knew what to say to Jack. There was no point in chastising him for running away. He'd shown no remorse when Howard had scolded him. She didn't want to offer false hope that his father would be arriving any minute, but it didn't seem right to try to prepare him for disappointment, either. So, Addy simply sat in the dim hallway with the children and said nothing.

She didn't know how much time had passed when the door across the hall opened and a curious neighbor peered out—a middle-aged woman with tired eyes and a faded kerchief on her head. She looked at Addy, then went back inside to drag out a chair for her. Two girls in their teens followed shyly.

"You like to sit?" the mother asked in accented English.

Addy accepted her kind offer. "Yes, thank you." The woman didn't seem to be in a hurry to leave, so Addy asked, "Did you know the family who used to live here?"

She nodded. "Krystyna. She Polski, like me."

"It was sad when she died," the older girl added in a soft voice.

"Did you know the children's father? He's supposed to be returning." The three shook their heads.

The two daughters spoke better English than their mother did, and Addy learned that all three of them worked in a garment factory and hadn't been home the day the authorities took Jack away. They had known Krystyna Thomas, who had emigrated from Poland like them, but knew nothing about Mr. Thomas except that he worked on a steamship. The two young sisters, Marta and Monika, were lovely girls, and Addy wished she could help them find better jobs, as she had helped Susannah. They deserved a better future than working long hours for low wages. But Addy's dream of starting a school for young women seemed a long way off.

More and more people began to gather in the hallway, talking with Addy and with each other, often in broken English, as they enjoyed Christmas Day off from work. Addy met a few more women who had known Jack's mother, and a man who had known his father.

At last, Howard strode through the tenement door with the carriage driver, their arms loaded down with baskets and boxes. Howard wore a broad grin on his face.

"What's all this?" Addy asked as he climbed the stairs.

"It's a Christmas feast! Is there someplace we can set it down?" Marta dashed inside her apartment and returned with a small table. "Thanks. But we're going to need a few more tables like that one!" He gestured to some of the children. "Can you give me a hand? Believe me, it will be worth your while."

"Howard, what is all this?" Addy asked again as he hauled another load up the stairs.

"Christmas dinner, darling. Between my mother and Mrs. Gleason, there's enough to feed an army. Knock on all the doors and invite everyone in the building to come and eat."

The aroma of ham and fresh rolls began to fill the hallway. More tables appeared, along with a few chairs for some of the elderly tenants. Mr. Pawloski came up from the basement, and even the elderly Russian woman who lived in Jack's old apartment joined them with her family. Addy couldn't believe the amount of food Howard had brought, including a ham dinner from his mother and a roasted turkey from Mrs. Gleason. There was a variety of bread and buns, potato dishes and vegetables, cakes, pies, cookies, and three fruit baskets. People brought out their own plates and utensils and dug into the feast. It reminded Addy of Christ's miracle of the loaves and fishes with enough food for all the neighbors to eat their fill.

"I helped make these cookies," Jack bragged to some of

the other boys. He was no longer on the floor, and seemed to be enjoying himself, laughing and racing around the hallways and stairs with the other boys. Polly played on the floor with two toddlers, showing them the wooden baby Jesus.

When the food was nearly gone, Howard opened several boxes of used clothing and shoes. "Merry Christmas, everyone! Take whatever you need." Marta found a pretty shirtwaist, and Monika a skirt. Judging by everyone's delight, Howard might have brought them the latest fashions from Paris. As the afternoon wore on, someone started singing Christmas carols, and everyone who knew the words joined in. Addy had attended many sumptuous Christmas balls, and feasted on elaborate Christmas dinners, but she couldn't recall a Christmas celebration more satisfying than this one.

By nightfall, no food remained. "Please, take everything but the pots and bowls," Howard urged, and they did, until not a crumb or a ham bone or a turkey bone remained. The unlit hallway grew dark after the sun set, and the warmth faded once all the people went back inside. Only Howard, Addy, and the children remained. Howard looked at his pocket watch, then gently took Jack by the shoulders and made him face him. "Listen, the carriage driver has been very generous to us today. He agreed to come back and bring us home to the town house, and he'll be here any minute. We need to go, now. All of us. These neighbors are our friends. They'll help your father find us."

Addy held her breath, wondering what Jack would do. She was relieved when he left without an argument, but his head hung very low.

CHAPTER 14

THE TOWN HOUSE WAS DARK and very chilly inside. Howard turned on the lights and went throughout the house, stoking all the fires. The children's sorrow and deep disappointment were painful to witness. The two of them huddled together on Howard's armchair, gazing out the front window into the darkened street.

"What now?" Addy whispered to Howard when he returned from his last trip to the coal bin.

He smiled half-heartedly and gestured to the wrapped presents beneath the tree. "Shall we open them?"

Addy agreed. "Jack, Polly, I think some of these presents have your names on them."

The children joined them without much enthusiasm, and all four of them sat on the floor beside the Christmas tree. Jack opened his presents carefully, as if afraid to tear the paper. Polly imitated him. His eyes brightened when he saw the fire engine. "This is really mine?" he asked.

"Yes, it's all yours," Howard replied.

Polly caressed her new doll's porcelain face, then hugged it to her chest, rocking it in her arms. She stood to put the wooden baby Jesus back in His manger, then sat down to cradle her doll again. Mrs. Gleason had knitted new hats and mittens for the children, and warm scarves for Addy and Howard. Susannah had helped Jack and Polly make pretty sachets with dried lavender for Addy's bureau drawers. Jack smiled when Addy praised them.

"They smell wonderful," she said inhaling the scent. "Thank you!"

The children had decorated a little wooden tray for Howard with his initials in bright, rainbow colors. "Susannah says you can put your keys and cuff links in it at night," Jack told him.

"She's right. This will be perfect for them. Thank you."

The presents that Addy and Howard had for each other remained, but she wanted to wait until they were alone to open them. She could feel the sadness begin to settle over their household again like fog, so she reached for Polly and pulled her onto her lap, suddenly certain about what she needed to do. "Jack, look at me," she said. He did, his eyes mournful. "I'm so very sorry that your father hasn't come. I know how sad you must feel. But I want you to know that you and Polly will have a home here with us, from now on. We won't send you back to the orphanage—or anywhere else." She put her arm around Jack and drew him closer, hugging both children as her tears fell.

Howard laid his hand on Jack's head for a moment as if in blessing, his own eyes shining with tears. "It happens to all of us that God sometimes doesn't answer our prayers the way we'd hoped," he said. "It doesn't mean He didn't hear you, or He's mad at you, or you did something wrong, but that He has something else planned for you. I know you're sad and disappointed, and you have every right to feel that way. You can pray and tell God exactly how you feel. He doesn't mind. But never stop trusting Him, Jack. Never doubt His love for you. I know Addy and I can never take the place of your parents, but the four of us can still be a family."

Jack threw himself into Howard's arms and sobbed, weeping for a long, long time. Addy felt Polly trembling with silent tears and wondered how much she understood. It must have been hard for her today to return to where she'd once lived. Did she understand that her parents were never coming back?

Eventually, the warmth of the fire and the events of the long day made everyone sleepy. Jack wanted to continue his vigil by the window and Addy didn't have the heart to send him downstairs to his room. They decided to let him stay there, and he finally fell asleep in the chair with Polly curled up beside him. Howard covered them with a blanket. "I'll carry them to bed when we're ready to go upstairs," he said. He drew a breath and looked at Addy as if afraid to speak.

"What's wrong?"

"Addy, I have to ask—are you sure about having Jack and Polly live here with us?"

"I'm very sure."

"What changed your mind?"

"I think it was seeing all those families in the tenement today." She paused, trying to put what she felt into words. "I've wanted to do big things for God, like my grandmother did. To make a difference, especially in the lives of women and children. People shouldn't have to live in poverty. They should have hope. That's why I joined the suffrage movement, and why I wanted to start a school for girls like Susannah. But when we shared that meal with those people today . . . It wasn't much to us, but it meant everything to them. And I realized that I can make a difference by doing simple, everyday things—like helping to raise two children."

"Addy, you've already made a difference in Susannah's life. And in Polly's and Jack's, too."

"Maybe that's all God asks of us. Some people are given the opportunity to do grand things in life, but if we just make a difference in the lives of the people God puts in our paths, I think He's pleased with that. Mrs. Gleason would say she's 'just a cook.' But she has blessed me, and my society friends, and Jack and Polly in more ways than I can count. She would say it wasn't much, but to us it was huge. I don't think it was a coincidence that Jack ended up on our doorstep. I believe God wanted us to help him."

Howard reached for her, pulling her into his arms as they sat together on the floor. "I love you so much."

"I love you, too." She wiped her eyes after they separated again. "But if the children are going to be ours, they can't keep sleeping in the maid's room," she said, laughing. "We must convince them to sleep upstairs in a proper bedroom."

Howard laughed, too, then said, "Hey, you haven't opened my present, Addy."

"I wanted to wait until we were alone. But I really want you to open mine, first. It's in those three boxes."

"What about these?" he asked, gesturing to three smaller packages.

"Those are for Jack's father."

Howard closed his eyes for a moment. "Oh."

"Jack was worried that his papa wouldn't have anything to open, so I told him that this one could be for him. It was supposed to be for you, but . . . and the other two presents are from Mrs. Gleason and the children."

The atmosphere had turned somber again. Howard sighed and reached for one of Addy's boxes. "All three are for me? Whoa, it's heavy!" He tore off the paper and opened the cardboard flaps. His eyes grew wide when he saw what was inside. He pulled out one beautiful, leatherbound volume after another, stroking the covers, opening them to sniff inside. "I love that smell! This is a treasure trove, Addy! I'm overwhelmed!"

"I saved some of the very best books from my family's library when my mother sold my great-grandfather's mansion. I spent a day going through the library with you in mind, remembering how much you admired all those volumes. They'll fit on these shelves in our parlor for now, but we can hire a carpenter later so you can start your very own library."

"They're wonderful, Addy. Thank you." He hugged her and kissed her again. "Now, open my present to you."

Addy untied the string and opened the plain brown wrapping paper to find a lawyer's accordion file, like the ones Howard used to bring to the mansion when he'd helped Mother settle Father's estate. She stared at it for a moment then smiled up at him. "This looks intriguing!" But before she had a chance to unwind the string clasp and open it, there was a loud banging on the front door. She and Howard stared at each other.

"Could it be?" he murmured. He scrambled to his feet before Addy could move, and raced to the door.

CHAPTER 15

ADDY HEARD HOWARD give a cry of joy. "You must be Mr. Thomas!"

"Are my children here?"

"Yes! Yes, they are!"

Addy sprang to her feet, her heart wild with excitement. Mr. Thomas was a stocky man in his early thirties with broad shoulders and a burly chest that threatened to pop the buttons off his woolen sea coat. His brown hair and beard were the same color as Jack's. He dropped his seabags inside the door and pushed past Howard, running toward Jack, who had awakened.

"Papa? Papa!"

Mr. Thomas lifted Jack from the chair, clutching him to his chest, whirling him around. The boy's laughter filled the room. "I knew you'd come, Papa! I just knew it!"

"Wild horses couldn't keep me away, son. I'm here, now. I'm here."

Tears blurred Addy's vision as she watched the joyful reunion. Howard closed the door and came to stand alongside her, wrapping his arm around her shoulder. "Can you believe this?" he asked. His voice sounded choked.

"No. It seems like a miracle!"

Jack's father set him down, then dropped to his knees in front of the chair. Tears coursed down his face and sparkled in his bushy beard as he pulled Polly into his arms. He tenderly held Polly's head against his chest and hummed a tune in his deep voice. Polly gave the widest smile Addy had ever seen as she clung to her papa.

"Merry Christmas, Mr. Thomas," Howard said. "Welcome home."

"Thank you. God bless you!" He rose and sank down in the chair as if too overcome to stand. The children scrambled onto his lap and he encircled them with his arms, his eyes squeezed tightly shut as if offering a silent prayer of thanks. Then he looked up at Howard and Addy. "God bless you for watching over my children. God bless you both."

"We're glad we could help," Addy said.

"Did you go to our house, Papa?" Jack asked. "Some lady is living in our house!"

"I know, son. And it's a very sad thing indeed." He gazed tenderly at his children as he spoke, touching their hair, their faces. "I went there first thing after my ship docked, and the new Russian family gave me this address. Then the family across the hall came to the door and told me you and Polly were just there earlier today with your friends."

"We had a big Christmas dinner while we were waiting for you, Papa."

"So I heard. Your friends are very generous people." He looked at Addy and Howard again and smiled.

"I'm so glad you found us," Addy said.

"It took some doing to get here—I walked part of the way and ran for a good bit until I finally found a fella with a carriage who was willing to help me out."

"I knew you would come home, Papa. I told everybody that you would, but no one believed me. They thought I was an orphan!"

"Jack never stopped believing and praying for your safe return," Addy said.

"And I lit a hundred Christmas candles."

Mr. Thomas ruffled Jack's hair, then kissed the top of his

head. He sighed as if carrying a terrible weight on his shoulders. "The neighbor told me about your mother." He pulled the children closer, rocking them, as if afraid he might lose them, too. A sob came from deep inside his chest. The room fell quiet for a moment.

"We've lost your mother, Jack, my boy. Our sweet, sweet Krystyna. I should have been there. I wish I had been. Now we've lost her."

"I'm so sorry, Mr. Thomas," Addy said.

He looked up at her and nodded, then turned back to the children. "But I promise I'll never go away again. Ever. I'll find a job here in the city and take care of you myself, from now on."

"I'll be happy to help you in any way that I can," Howard said.

"Me, too." Addy's mind was already racing with thoughts of how she could help the family get back on their feet. Howard could try to help Mr. Thomas find a job, and maybe she and Mrs. Gleason could watch little Polly while he was at work and Jack was at school.

"Hey, you gotta open your Christmas presents, Papa!" Jack said suddenly. He slid off his father's lap and retrieved the presents from beneath the tree. Addy watched as he opened them. The leather gloves—Howard's gloves—fit him perfectly.

So did the hat Mrs. Gleason had knit. The children had made him a little tray like Howard's but with their handprints on it.

"Ah, this is wonderful, Jack. Thank you." He planted a kiss on each of the children's cheeks. "Now, I have a little something for you, too. Fetch my bag for me, son. The smaller one." Jack hurried to the front doorway where his papa had dropped his seabags. He strained as he lugged it into the parlor. "Aye, that's it." Mr. Thomas unbuckled the straps and pulled out a little stuffed bear with shiny button eyes for Polly. She smiled with delight and rubbed the soft fur against her cheek. Jack's eyes went wide when he saw the folding pocketknife his papa had brought him.

"This is mine?"

"Yep. I'll show you how to use it, son. But be careful, it's sharp." Next, he pulled out a cigar box filled with more than a dozen finely-carved wooden animals.

"Wow! You made these, Papa?" Jack fingered a plump bear while Polly reached for a little cat.

"Aye, just for you and Polly. I'll teach you how to whittle and you can make them, too." He watched his children examine their gifts, and it seemed as though he never wanted to stop gazing at them. Then he looked up at Addy and Howard and said, "How can I ever thank you for taking such good care of them for me?"

"There's no need, Mr. Thomas. We enjoyed having them."

"Please, call me Rob."

Addy watched them for another moment before asking, "Are you hungry, Rob? Can I fix you something to eat?" Then she suddenly remembered the mounds of food at the tenement and gasped. "Oh no! Is there anything left in our pantry, Howard?"

"I'm sure we can find something," he said, laughing.

They moved downstairs to the kitchen. Howard made coffee and fried some bacon while Addy scrambled eggs. Rob sat at the kitchen table to eat with a child on each knee. Jack had his arm around his papa's burly shoulder while Polly stroked his soft beard. All three of them seemed reluctant to let the others out of their sight.

"You were gone a long time, Papa," Jack said. "Where did you go?"

"Well, we picked up cargo in the Caribbean, first," he said, talking between bites, "then crossed the sea to Liverpool. We hopped between quite a few ports over there, places like Rotterdam and Hamburg, then finally returned to New York. I never should have gone away at all," he said, shaking his head. "But your mama and I decided that I could make more money working on a ship, and then we could afford a doctor." He looked up at Addy and Howard, who were seated across the table. "Krystyna had rheumatic fever as a girl and it weakened her heart. That's probably why the dysentery killed her."

"We're so sorry, Rob. Your neighbors at the tenement spoke very highly of her."

"She was a good woman, and a wonderful mother. She didn't care about hiring a doctor for herself, but she'd hoped that we could find one who could help Polly. She had a very high fever when she was a year old, and after that we noticed that she couldn't hear anymore."

"I know a doctor we can ask to examine her," Addy said. "Dr. Matthew Murphy was a friend of my grandmother."

"I would be very grateful. Krystyna and I talked it over," Rob said as he continued to eat. "And we decided that I would go to sea one last time. But it meant I would be away for months. I never would have gone if I'd known that I'd never see her again." His voice choked to a whisper.

"She's in heaven with Jesus and the angels, right?" Jack asked.

Rob cleared his throat. "Aye, she most certainly is. We'll see her again, someday. But, oh, how we will miss her until then." He hugged his children again. "I thank God that I didn't lose Jack and Polly, too. Pawloski told me that I would have lost them forever, if it hadn't been for the two of you. I owe you a lot. I'll never be able to repay you."

"It's mostly thanks to Jack," Howard said. "He came to us for help and wouldn't give up until we found Polly and you. He's a remarkable boy."

"We tried to find other family members," Addy said, "but had no luck."

"No, my wife immigrated here with her parents, who have both died. All her other relatives are back in Poland. I'm originally from Baltimore, but I left a bad homelife when I was thirteen. I worked on ships, traveling the seas, until I met Krystyna. She and her parents were steerage passengers."

He had finished his meal, and he thanked them again for the food. "Do you want a cookie, Papa?" Jack asked. "Polly and I helped bake them."

"Um, I think they're all gone, Jack," Addy said. "We shared them at the tenement house, remember?"

"There's still some on the Christmas tree," he said. "I'll go get them." He sprinted up the stairs to the parlor and returned with three gingerbread men. Addy thought they might be a little stale by now, but she hid a smile as Rob, Jack, and Polly crunched into them.

The children were yawning again by the time the cookies were gone. Addy convinced the family to sleep in the upstairs bedroom, and hurried to get the room ready for them, carrying blankets and pillows from the tiny servants' room. She and Howard said goodnight and went back down to the parlor, leaving the little family to themselves. Addy gazed at the lopsided tree and the scattered wrappings and presents while Howard tended the stoves for the night. She felt dazed by everything that had happened tonight, yet filled with joy.

"I think we just witnessed a miracle," she murmured.

"I agree. This would have ended in disaster if Jack hadn't had the courage to stow away in your mother's carriage."

"I shudder when I think of Jack living in the orphanage and Polly in that horrible asylum. And their papa never knowing what happened to them. Thank you for helping me search for them, Howard. You're my hero." She brushed a streak of soot from his cheek before going into his arms.

"You worked just as hard as I did, darling."

"You know, when I saw Rob being reunited with his children tonight it helped me understand Christmas in a new way."

"How's that?"

"What our heavenly Father wants more than anything else is to be reunited with His lost children. That's why He sent Jesus."

CHAPTER 16

"I KNOW WE SHOULD probably go to bed after such an eventful day," Addy said, "but I'm not even sleepy. I'm just . . . overwhelmed! I feel like I'm in a dream!"

"It has been quite a day."

"You hauled all that food across town," she said, laughing, "but the neighbors in the tenement were so grateful, weren't they?"

"Maybe we should make it a yearly event."

"I like that idea. Your mother and Mrs. Gleason are amazing. Wait until we tell them about all the people they fed today!"

Howard gestured to the paper-strewn floor and smiled. "Hey, you didn't finish opening your present from me."

Addy knelt and unwound the string clasp. Inside the file were what looked like legal documents. "What is all this?"

Howard reached to help her to her feet. "We'll have to take a little walk for me to show you. Would you mind a short walk? Or would you rather wait until morning?"

She saw his expression of joy and anticipation, and laughed. "There is no chance at all that I'm waiting!" He helped her with her coat and they stepped out into the dark night. A light snow was falling, but they wrapped the new scarves from Mrs. Gleason around their necks to keep warm. They walked for about two blocks, holding onto each other to keep from slipping in the fresh snow, then turned down a pleasant street lined with stores—a grocery, a fruit market, a cobbler's shop. They were closed for the night, but lights glowed in the apartments above the store fronts. A large stone house sat alone at the end of the block, the windows dark. A *For Sale* sign hung in the front window. Howard stopped in front of it.

"The file I gave you contains all the paperwork necessary to purchase this house for your girls' school."

"W-what?" She stared at him in disbelief, then up at the darkened building. It seemed out of place among the newer storefronts on the street, as if dropped out of heaven, just for her. It didn't seem to be in disrepair, and was a good size—a solid, two-story stone house that could accommodate classrooms and maybe even a dormitory. It was exactly the way she had pictured her dream school, and her mind raced with all the possibilities it offered.

"Oh, Howard! It's beautiful!"

"I'm glad you like it. I was able to negotiate a good price from the sellers, especially after they learned why you wanted it. All you need to do is tour the house, and if you think it will suit, you can sign the papers. It will be yours."

Addy turned to look up at him. "But . . . but how? Does this mean you agree to spend our inheritance to buy it?"

Howard nodded. "I learned a little bit about faith and hope these past few weeks. You were right, Addy, about trusting God for our future. We should do all the good we can right now instead of hoarding our money."

She closed her eyes and hugged him tightly. "Now I'm certain I'm dreaming!"

"I should also add that you won't have to spend all your inheritance on the school," he said when they parted again. "The wives of three of the partners in my firm—who happen to support women's suffrage—also love your idea and want to help create an endowment to fund it. Some of the paperwork I gave you will register it as a nonprofit organization. I think you can probably persuade the Stanhope Foundation to contribute, as well."

"You did all this for me?"

"Your school is a wonderful idea, Addy. I want to support you any way I can. And since arranging legal paperwork is what I do . . ."

"It's a wonderful gift, Howard. It's perfect!" She couldn't stop staring at the darkened building, imagining it full of light and bursting with young women who longed to improve their lives.

"I didn't think you'd want a sapphire necklace or a diamond ring."

Addy smiled. "You know me very well."

"I'd hoped we could tour the house today—I have a key—but it will have to wait until daylight."

"All right. We'd better go home now, before my tears freeze to my face," she said, wiping them.

Howard held her close to his side again as they started walking. The gentle snow continued to fall, turning the dark streets white. "This has been the most unusual Christmas Day I've ever had," he said.

"For me, too. Yet this is what Christmas is truly about,

isn't it? Loving our neighbor. Spreading God's love to others. And bringing the lost ones home."

"Well said, darling Addy. Merry Christmas."

"It's the merriest Christmas ever!"

A Note from the Author

Dear Reader,

The very heart of Christmas is God's longing for His children to be reunited with Him. It's why He sent His Son on the first Christmas. Jesus said, "the Son of Man came to seek and to save the lost" (Luke 19:10). Many of us have friends and loved ones who've wandered away from God. What better time than Christmas to light a hundred candles and say a hundred prayers for them to come home to our heavenly Father. As you count the weeks to Christmas, let the Advent candles remind you of the hope, love, joy, and peace that are ours when we know Jesus.

Thankfully, the US no longer has orphanages overflowing with destitute children as there were in the last century. But there are still children, both here and around the world, who long for loving families and who need to hear the message of God's love. Here are a few organizations that I'm happy to support, which reach out to children:

Prison Fellowship Angel Tree (prisonfellowship.org) buys Christmas gifts for the children of prisoners.

Samaritan's Purse (samaritanspurse.org) gives shoeboxes filled with gifts and the Gospel story to children around the world through its Operation Christmas Child program.

Toys For Tots (toysfortots.org) operated by the U.S. Marine Corps, collects gifts for needy children.

World Vision (worldvision.org) lets you sponsor a child from an impoverished country, providing food, an education, and the hope of the Gospel.

I hope you've enjoyed reading the continuation of Addy and Howard's story, which began in my novel *All My Secrets*. May you and your family enjoy this blessed season of giving.

Merry Christmas!
Lynn

Discussion Questions

1. If you have read *All My Secrets*, did you enjoy seeing Addy and Howard again? Did anything about their life together surprise you? If you haven't read the novel yet, did this story pique your interest in learning more of the characters' backgrounds?

2. Before reading this book, how much did you know about the conditions of orphans around the turn of the twentieth century? How is the treatment of vulnerable children better now? Where is there still room for improvement?

3. Howard and Addy face a challenge common to many newlyweds: figuring out how to merge their finances. Why is Howard so adamant about not using Addy's inheritance? Why does Addy disagree? How are the financial challenges facing young couples today similar or different?

4. Addy is passionate about women's rights—not just the right to vote, but also having access to higher education, better job opportunities, and higher wages. How are American women's lives better than they were a century ago, thanks to the efforts of crusaders like Addy? What further changes might still be necessary?

5. Howard and Addy first fear that Jack's father intentionally abandoned his family. What did you think of the way this story thread is resolved?

6. At first, reports about Jack's young sister seem to suggest that she might have a mental impairment. Were you surprised when you learned the truth about her?

7. In the end, Howard and Addy agree on using her inheritance in a way that will honor the memory of Addy's grandmother. Do you feel it's important to honor our parents and grandparents in how we use our resources?

8. What are some of the Christmas traditions observed in the book? How have Christmas traditions changed since the time this book was set, and in what ways are they still pretty much the same? What are some of your family's traditions?

About the Author

LYNN AUSTIN has sold nearly two and a half million copies of her books worldwide. A former teacher who now writes and speaks full-time, she has won eight Christy Awards for her historical fiction and was one of the first inductees into the Christy Award Hall of Fame. One of her novels, *Hidden Places*, was made into a Hallmark Channel Original Movie. Lynn and her husband have three grown children and make their home in western Michigan. Visit her online at lynnaustin.org.

Step back in time again with these historicals from Lynn Austin

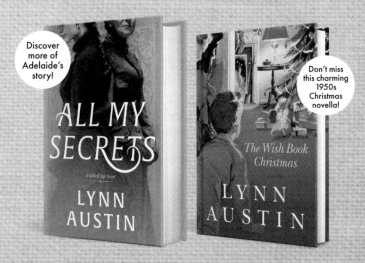

Discover more of Adelaide's story!

Don't miss this charming 1950s Christmas novella!

AVAILABLE NOW IN STORES AND ONLINE

CONNECT WITH LYNN ONLINE AT

lynnaustin.org

OR FOLLOW HER ON:

f @LynnAustinBooks

X @LynnNAustin

g @Lynn_Austin

CP1586